# TEN TOP STORIES

### Selected by
## DAVID A. SOHN

BANTAM  BOOKS

BANTAM PATHFINDER EDITIONS

NEW YORK / TORONTO / LONDON

RLI: $\dfrac{\text{VLM } 5}{\text{IL } 7.12}$

TEN TOP STORIES

*Bantam Pathfinder edition published November 1964*
*2nd printing*
*3rd printing*
*4th printing*
*5th printing*
*6th printing*
*7th printing*
*8th printing*

### ACKNOWLEDGEMENTS

"Flowers for Algernon" by Daniel Keyes, reprinted from THE MAGA-
ZINE OF FANTASY AND SCIENCE FICTION by permission of Mercury
Press Inc. and Robert Mills, agent. Copyright © 1959 by Daniel
Keyes.
"So Much Unfairness of Things" by C. D. B. Bryan, reprinted from
THE NEW YORKER Magazine Inc. by permission of Brandt and Brandt.
Copyright © 1962 The New Yorker Magazine Inc. The version ap-
pearing in this volume has been edited with the permission of Brandt
and Brandt.
"Backward Boy" by Gene Coghlan, reprinted from THE SATURDAY
EVENING POST by permission of the Curtis Publishing Company and
the author. Copyright © 1960, The Curtis Publishing Company.
"Denton's Daughter" by Ellen Lowenberg, reprinted from SEVEN-
TEEN by permission of SEVENTEEN and the author. Copyright © 1963
by SEVENTEEN.
"Hoods I Have Known" by Sondra Spatt, reprinted from MADEMOI-
SELLE by permission of Street and Smith Publications, Inc., and the
author. Copyright © 1956 by Street and Smith Publications, Inc.
"Planet of the Condemned" by Robert Murphy, reprinted from THE
SATURDAY EVENING POST by permission of the Curtis Publishing Com-
pany and Harold Ober Associates Incorporated. Copyright © 1960
by the Curtis Publishing Company.
"Test" by Theodore L. Thomas, reprinted from THE MAGAZINE OF
FANTASY AND SCIENCE FICTION by permission of Mercury Press Inc.
and the author. Copyright © 1962 by Mercury Press Inc.
"See How They Run" by George Harmon Coxe, reprinted by per-
mission of Brandt and Brandt. Copyright © 1941 by the Curtis
Publishing Company.
"Polar Night" by Norah Burke, reprinted by permission of Whit
Burnett and Hallie Burnett from STORY No. 4. Copyright © 1953
by Whit Burnett and Hallie Burnett.
"The Turtle" by George Vukelich, reprinted from THE UNIVERSITY
OF KANSAS CITY REVIEW by permission of THE UNIVERSITY OF KAN-
SAS CITY REVIEW and the author. Copyright © 1959 by THE UNI-
VERSITY OF KANSAS CITY REVIEW.

*Library of Congress Catalog Card Number: 64-25021*

*All rights reserved.*
*Copyright © 1964 by Bantam Books, Inc.*
*Published simultaneously in the*
*United States and Canada.*

*Bantam Books are published by Bantam Books, Inc. Its trade-mark,
consisting of the words "Bantam Books" and the portrayal of a
bantam, is registered in the United States Patent Office and in other
countries. Marca Registrada. Printed in the United States of America. Bantam Books, Inc., 271 Madison Ave., New York 16, N. Y.*

# CONTENTS

# INTRODUCTION

These stories are intended to appeal to young adults, one of the hardest groups to please. Readers between twelve and twenty are fierce, discriminating critics of short stories that must pass the tests of both interest and quality. If a tale bores a teenager, he drops it, and if asked, he tells you why. Teenagers react to literature in much the same way that they react to parents, teachers, and other symbols of authority. Their candid reactions make an excellent proving ground for the writer, but he must be willing to submit to brutal scrutiny and accept the impatient rule: "One strike and you're out!"

*Ten Top Stories* is the result of a long experience with many stories that struck out and a few that survived. Ten times the number of stories in this volume were seriously considered for it, after countless numbers of others were read in a search for tales that would both interest students and contain the mysterious elements which make a story worth reading. The editor was often fooled by stories that seemed "tailor-made" for this group but, happily, students to whom they were read quickly spotted vapidity of style, false characterization, and any other phony, expedient element. Writers who patronized the reader were rejected in short order, and justifiably so. Thus these stories have passed a fiery test of student appraisal; they stand on top of a mountain of other tales that were blasted out of the running for one good reason or another.

This collection also attempts to provide fresh talent for the reader. Though some of these stories have appeared in specialized hardcover anthologies, none of them can be called "old chestnuts." And the editor hopes that they will retain the sparkle and punch that earlier readers found in them.

Variety and balance are vital considerations in a short-story anthology. The readers of *Ten Top Stories* will find in various places humor, pathos, fantasy, realism, adventure, cruelty, compassion, love, and death. These are stories about astronauts, brilliant people, retarded children, juvenile delinquents, animals, athletes, scientists, and others. Problems in the stories are sometimes serious, sometimes trivial, and often unusual. The young adult reader should find it easy to identify himself with the characters in these stories and in the situations they face.

That every story should please every person who reads it would be miraculous. Obviously this cannot be expected; but most of these stories should satisfy the reading tastes of the typical young adult. At least some of them will prove to be vivid, moving experiences for him.

The following brief descriptions will give the reader some knowledge of the scope and nature of this anthology:

FLOWERS FOR ALGERNON by Daniel Keyes This remarkable story won the Hugo Award, the highest annual award given to a story of fantasy and science fiction. Written in diary form, it concerns a young man, Charlie Gordon, who is intellectually retarded. Charlie is made the subject of a scientific experiment to increase intelligence in human beings.

It has been a successful television play, a movie based on it is planned, and Daniel Keyes intends to convert it into a novel.

SO MUCH UNFAIRNESS OF THINGS by C. D. B. Bryan This is the story of a student in a private school who is faced with the problem of whether or not to cheat on an examination. The atmosphere of the private school and the tension of the examination are created with great power and skill by the author. An extremely vivid reading experience, reflecting an unusual writing talent.

BACKWARD BOY by Gene Coghlan  Gene Coghlan, who presently lives in Alaska, has created a memorable character in Auber, the backward boy. This story was selected as one of the best from *The Saturday Evening Post* during the year it was published.

DENTON'S DAUGHTER by Ellen Lowenberg  One of the winners of the *Seventeen* writing awards contest, this is an appealing, humorous story about a student who tries to resolve a conflict between good marks and the girl he loves.

HOODS I HAVE KNOWN by Sondra Spatt  This story was selected as one of the best from *Mademoiselle*, in its anthology of good stories of the past several years. Its narrator describes, with skilful humor and style, her fleeting relationship with Danny Tooey, the hood of the class, when she is forced to sit next to him at the back of the room.

PLANET OF THE CONDEMNED by Robert Murphy  In an absorbing science-fiction story about astronauts searching for a previously undiscovered planet, the author has combined a keen sense of plot structure with a talent for characterization and realistic detail to form a hair-raising tale that has a jolting surprise ending. Also selected as one of the best stories from the *Post* during the year it was published.

TEST by Theodore L. Thomas  An imaginative fantasy in which the author raises an important question about young automobile drivers. This is a story that unites economy of style with an adept knowledge of the use of the unexpected ending. It provokes a great deal of thought from the reader about responsibility.

SEE HOW THEY RUN by George Harmon Coxe  Most sports stories are about popular sports such as baseball, basketball, and football. This, however, is a story about a long-distance runner that makes the reader feel as if he has run the race right along with Johnny Burke. The situation, characterization, and style of writing separate it from the ordinary sports story that depends on plot alone.

POLAR NIGHT by Norah Burke  Stories told from the point of view of an animal are difficult to write, but the author of this story skilfully relates the struggle of a polar bear and her cubs against the cruelty of man and nature in the Arctic. The reader, along with these animals, experiences the rugged polar night and its dangers in this artfully constructed story.

THE TURTLE by George Vukelich  Another animal story which is simple on the surface, this is also a comment on human nature, expressed with skill and subtlety.

As you can see, various themes and relationships are apparent in this collection. To what extent should science affect the lives of individuals? How considerate are we to people less fortunate than ourselves? When is the will to succeed constructive? When is it a destructive influence?

There are few pleasures that compare to reading a story well told, and when the reader gains greater understanding of his world, his fellow creatures, and himself, it is the precious dividend that excellent writers offer him. To provide such reading enjoyment is the wish of the editor and the purpose of this anthology.

DAVID A. SOHN

# FLOWERS FOR ALGERNON

## BY DANIEL KEYES

📖 📖 📖

### progris riport 1—martch 5, 1965

Dr. Strauss says I shud rite down what I think and evrey thing that happins to me from now on. I dont know why but he says its importint so they will see if they will use me. I hope they use me. Miss Kinnian says maybe they can make me smart. I want to be smart. My name is Charlie Gordon. I am 37 years old. I have nuthing more to rite now so I will close for today.

### progris riport 2—martch 6

I had a test today. I think I faled it. And I think maybe now they wont use me. What happind is a nice young man was in the room and he had some white cards and ink spillled all over them. He sed Charlie what do yo see on this card. I was very skared even tho I had my rabits foot in my pockit because when I was a kid I always faled tests in school and I spillled ink to.

I told him I saw a inkblot. He said yes and it made me feel good. I thot that was all but when I got up to go he said Charlie we are not thru yet. Then I dont remember so good but he wantid me to say what was in the ink. I dint see nuthing in the ink but he said there was picturs there other pepul saw some picturs. I couldnt see any picturs. I reely tryed. I held the card close up and then far away. Then I said if I had my glases I coud see better ter I usally only ware my glases in the movies or TV but I said they are in the closit in the hall. I got them. Then I said let me see that card agen I bet Ill find it now.

I tryed hard but I only saw the ink. I told him maybe I need new glases. He rote something down on a paper and I got skared of faling the test. I told him it was

5

a very nice inkblot with littel points all around the edges.
He looked very sad so that wasnt it. I said please let me
try agen. Ill get it in a few minits becaus Im not so fast
somtimes. Im a slow reeder too in Miss Kinnians class for
slow adults but I'm trying very hard.

He gave me a chance with another card that had 2
kinds of ink spilled on it red and blue.

He was very nice and talked slow like Miss Kinnian
does and he explaned it to me that it was a *raw shok*. He
said pepul see things in the ink. I said show me where.
He said think. I told him I think a inkblot but that wasn't
rite eather. He said what does it remind you—pretend
something. I closed my eyes for a long time to pretend. I
told him I pretend a fowntan pen with ink leeking all over
a table cloth.

I dont think I passed the *raw shok* test

**progris riport 3—martch 7**

Dr Strauss and Dr Nemur say it dont matter about the
inkblots. They said that maybe they will still use me. I
said Miss Kinnian never gave me tests like that one only
spelling and reading. They said Miss Kinnian told that I
was her bestist pupil in the adult nite school becaus I
tryed the hardist and I reely wantid to lern. They said
how come you went to the adult nite scool all by yourself Charlie. How did you find it. I said I asked pepul
and sumbody told me where I shud go to lern to read and
spell good. They said why did you want to. I told them
becaus all my life I wantid to be smart and not dumb.
But its very hard to be smart. They said you know it will
probly be tempirery. I said yes. Miss Kinnian told me. I
dont care if it herts.

Later I had more crazy tests today. The nice lady who
gave it to me told me the name and I asked her how do
you spellit so I can rite it my progris riport. THEMATIC
APPERCEPTION TEST. I dont know the frist 2 words
but I know what *test* means. You got to pass it or you get
bad marks. This test lookd easy becaus I coud see the
picturs. Only this time she dint want me to tell her the

picturs. That mixd me up. She said make up storys about the pepul in the picturs.

I told her how can you tell storys about pepul you never met. I said why shud I make up lies. I never tell lies any more becaus I always get caut.

She told me this test and the other one the raw-shok was for getting personality. I laffed so hard. I said how can you get that thing from inkblots and fotos. She got sore and put her picturs away. I don't care. It was sily. I gess I faled that test too.

Later some men in white coats took me to a difernt part of the hospitil and gave me a game to play. It was like a race with a white mouse. They called the mouse Algernon. Algernon was in a box with a lot of twists and turns like all kinds of walls and they gave me a pencil and a paper with lines and lots of boxes. On one side it said START and on the other end it said FINISH. They said it was *amazed* and that Algernon and me had the same *amazed* to do. I dint see how we could have the same *amazed* if Algernon had a box and I had a paper but I dint say nothing. Anyway there wasnt time because the race started.

One of the men had a watch he was trying to hide so I wouldnt see it so I tryed not to look and that made me nervus.

Anyway that test made me feel worser than all the others because they did it over 10 times with different *amazeds* and Algernon won every time. I dint know that mice were so smart. Maybe thats because Algernon is a white mouse. Maybe white mice are smarter than other mice.

### progris riport 4—Mar 8

Their going to use me! Im so exited I can hardly write. Dr Nemur and Dr Strauss had a argament about it first. Dr Nemur was in the office when Dr Strauss brot me in. Dr Nemur was worryed about using me but Dr Strauss told him Miss Kinnian rekemmended me the best from all the people who she was teaching. I like Miss Kinnian becaus shes a very smart teacher. And she said Charlie your going to have a second chance. If you volenteer for this experament you mite get smart. They dont know if it will be perminint but theirs a chance. Thats why I said ok even when I was scared because she said it was an operashun. She said dont be scared Charlie you done so much with so little I think you deserv it most of all.

So I got scaird when Dr. Nemur and Dr. Strauss argud about it. Dr. Strauss said I had something that was very good. He said I had a good *motorvation*. I never even knew I had that. I felt proud when he said that not every body with an eye-q of 68 had that thing. I dont know what it is or where I got it but he said Algernon had it too. Algernons *motor-vation* is the cheese they put in his box. But it cant be that because I didn't eat any cheese this week.

Then he told Dr Nemur something I dint understand so while they were talking I wrote down some of the words.

He said Dr. Nemur I know Charlie is not what you had in mind as the first of your new brede of intelek* * (coudnt get the word) superman. But most people of his low ment* * are host* * and uncoop* * they are usually dull apath* * and hard to reach. He has a good natcher hes intristed and eager to please.

Dr Nemur said remember he will be the first human beeng ever to have his intellijence tripled by surgicle meens.

Dr. Strauss said exakly. Look at how well hes lerned to read and write for his low mentel age its as grate an acheve* * as you and I lerning einstines therey of * *vity without help. That shows the inteness motor-vation. Its comparat* * a tremen* * achev* * I say we use Charlie.

I dint get all the words but it sounded like Dr Strauss was on my side and like the other one wasnt.

Then Dr Nemur nodded he said all right maybe your right. We will use Charlie. When he said that I got so exited I jumped up and shook his hand for being so good to me. I told him thank you doc you wont be sorry for giving me a second chance. And I mean it like I told him. After the operashun Im gonna try to be smart. Im gonna try awful hard.

## progris riport 5—Mar 10

Im skared. Lots of the nurses and the people who gave me the tests came to bring me candy and wish me luck. I hope I have luck. I got my rabits foot and my lucky penny. Only a black cat crossed me when I was comming to the hospitil. Dr Strauss says dont be supersitis Charlie this is science. Anyway Im keeping my rabits foot with me.

I asked Dr Strauss if Ill beat Algernon in the race after the operashun and he said maybe. If the operashun works Ill show that mouse I can be as smart as he is. Maybe smarter. Then Ill be abel to read better and spell the words good and know lots of things and be like other people. I want to be smart like other people. If it works perminint they will make everybody smart all over the wurld.

They dint give me anything to eat this morning. I dont know what that eating has to do with getting smart. Im very hungry and Dr. Nemur took away my box of candy. That Dr Nemur is a grouch. Dr Strauss says I can have it back after the operashun. You cant eat befor a operashun . . .

## progress report 6—Mar 15

The operashun dint hurt. He did it while I was sleeping. They took off the bandijis from my head today so I can make a PROGRESS REPORT. Dr. Nemur who looked at some of my other ones says I spell PROGRESS wrong and told me how to spell it and REPORT too. I got to try and remember that.

I have a very bad memary for spelling. Dr Strauss says its ok to tell about all the things that happin to me but he says I should tell more about what I feel and what I think. When I told him I dont know how to think he said try. All the time when the bandijis were on my eyes I tryed to think. Nothing happened. I dont

know what to think about. Maybe if I ask him he will
tell me how I can think now that Im suppose to get
smart. What do smart people think about. Fancy things
I suppose. I wish I knew some fancy things alredy.

### progress report 7—mar 19

Nothing is happining. I had lots of tests and different
kinds of races with Algernon. I hate that mouse. He
always beats me. Dr. Strauss said I got to play those
games. And he said some time I got to take those tests
over again. Those inkblots are stupid. And those pictures are stupid too. I like to draw a picture of a man
and a woman but I wont make up lies about people.

I got a headache from trying to think so much. I
thot Dr Strauss was my frend but he dont help me.
He dont tell me what to think or when Ill get smart.
Miss Kinnian dint come to see me. I think writing these
progress reports are stupid too.

### progress report 8—Mar 23

Im going back to work at the factory. They said it
was better I shud go back to work but I cant tell anyone what the operashun was for and I have to come
to the hospitil for an hour evry night after work. They
are gonna pay me mony every month for learning to
be smart.

Im glad Im going back to work because I miss my
job and all my frends and all the fun we have there.

Dr Strauss says I shud keep writing things down but
I dont have to do it every day just when I think of
something or something speshul happins. He says dont
get discoridged because it takes time and it happins slow.
He says it took a long time with Algernon before he got
3 times smarter than he was before. Thats why Algernon
beats me all the time because he had that operashun
too. That makes me feel better. I coud probly do that
*amazed* faster than a reglar mouse. Maybe some day
Ill beat him. That would be something. So far Algernon
looks smart perminent.

*Mar* 25   (I dont have to write PROGRESS REPORT on top any more just when I hand it in once a week for Dr Nemur. I just have to put the date on. That saves time)

We had a lot of fun at the factery today. Joe Carp said hey look where Charlie had his operashun what did they do Charlie put some brains in. I was going to tell him but I remembered Dr Strauss said no. Then Frank Reilly said what did you do Charlie forget your key and open your door the hard way. That made me laff. Their really my friends and they like me.

Sometimes somebody will say hey look at Joe or Frank or George he really pulled a Charlie Gordon. I dont know why they say that but they always laff. This morning Amos Borg who is the 4 man at Donnegans used my name when he shouted at Ernie the office boy. Ernie lost a packige. He said Ernie for godsake what are you trying to be a Charlie Gordon. I dont understand why he said that.

*Mar* 28   Dr Strauss came to my room tonight to see why I dint come in like I was suppose to. I told him I dont like to race with Algernon any more. He said I dont have to for a while but I shud come in. He had a present for me. I thot it was a little television but it wasnt. He said I got to turn it on when I go to sleep. I said your kidding why shud I turn it on when Im going to sleep. Who ever herd of a thing like that. But he said if I want to get smart I got to do what he says. I told him I dint think I was going to get smart and he puts his hand on my sholder and said Charlie you dont know it yet but your getting smarter all the time. You wont notice for a while. I think he was just being nice to make me feel good because I dont look any smarter.

Oh yes I almost forgot. I asked him when I can go back to the class at Miss Kinnians school. He said I wont go their. He said that soon Miss Kinnian will come to the hospitil to start and teach me speshul.

*Mar* 29   That crazy TV kept up all night. How can
I sleep with something yelling crazy things all night in
my ears. And the nutty pictures. Wow. I don't know
what it says when Im up so how am I going to know
when Im sleeping.

Dr Strauss says its ok. He says my brains are lerning
when I sleep and that will help me when Miss Kinnian
starts my lessons in the hospitl (only I found out it
isn't a hospitil its a labatory.) I think its all crazy.
If you can get smart when your sleeping why do people
go to school. That thing I don't think will work. I use
to watch the late show and the late late show on TV
all the time and it never made me smart. Maybe you
have to sleep while you watch it.

**progress report 9—April 3**
Dr Strauss showed me how to keep the TV turned
low so now I can sleep. I don't hear a thing. And I
still dont understand what it says. A few times I play
it over in the morning to find out what I lerned when
I was sleeping and I don't think so. Miss Kinnian says
Maybe its another langwidge. But most times it sounds
american. It talks faster than even Miss Gold who was
my teacher in 6 grade.

I told Dr. Strauss what good is it to get smart in my
sleep. I want to be smart when Im awake. He says its
the same thing and I have two minds. Theres the *subconscious* and the *conscious* (thats how you spell it).
And one dont tell the other one what its doing. They
dont even talk to each other. Thats why I dream. And
boy have I been having crazy dreams. Wow. Ever since
that night TV. The late late late show.

I forgot to ask him if it was only me or if everybody had those two minds.

(I just looked up the word in the dictionary Dr Strauss
gave me. The word is *subconscious. adj. Of the nature of
mental operations yet not present in consciousness; as,
subconscious conflict of desires.*) There's more but I
still dont know what it means. This isnt a very good
dictionary for dumb people like me.

Anyway the headache is from the party. My friends from the factery Joe Carp and Frank Reilly invited me to go to Muggsys Saloon for some drinks. I don't like to drink but they said we will have lots of fun. I had a good time.

Joe Carp said I shoud show the girls how I mop out the toilet in the factory and he got me a mop. I showed them and everyone laffed when I told that Mr. Donnegan said I was the best janiter he ever had because I like my job and do it good and never miss a day except for my operashun.

I said Miss Kinnian always said Charlie be proud of your job because you do it good.

Everybody laffed and we had a good time and they gave me lots of drinks and Joe said Charlie is a card when hes potted. I dont know what that means but everybody likes me and we have fun. I cant wait to be smart like my best friends Joe Carp and Frank Reilly.

I dont remember how the party was over but I think I went out to buy a newspaper and coffe for Joe and Frank and when I came back there was no one their. I looked for them all over till late. Then I dont remember so good but I think I got sleepy or sick. A nice cop brot me back home Thats what my landlady Mrs Flynn says.

But I got a headache and a big lump on my head. I think maybe I fell but Joe Carp says it was the cop they beat up drunks some times. I don't think so. Miss Kinnian says cops are to help people. Anyway I got a bad headache and Im sick and hurt all over. I dont think Ill drink anymore.


*April 6* I beat Algernon! I dint even know I beat him until Burt the tester told me. Then the second time I lost because I got so exited I fell off the chair before I finished. But after that I beat him 8 more times. I must be getting smart to beat a smart mouse like Algernon. But I don't *feel* smarter.

I wanted to race Algernon some more but Burt said thats enough for one day. They let me hold him for a

minit. Hes not so bad. Hes soft like a ball of cotton.
He blinks and when he opens his eyes their black and
pink on the eges.

I said can I feed him because I felt bad to beat him
and I wanted to be nice and make friends. Burt said
no Algernon is a very specshul mouse with an operashun like mine, and he was the first of all the animals
to stay smart so long. He told me Algernon is so smart
that every day he has to solve a test to get his food.
Its a thing like a lock on a door that changes every
time Algernon goes in to eat so he has to lern something new to get his food. That made me sad because
if he couldn't lern he woud be hungry.

I don't think its right to make you pass a test to eat.
How would Dr Nemur like it to have to pass a test
every time he wants to eat. I think Ill be friends with
Algernon.

*April* 9    Tonight after work Miss Kinnian was at the
laboratory. She looked like she was glad to see me but
scared. I told her dont worry Miss Kinnian Im not smart
yet and she laffed. She said I have confidence in you
Charlie the way you struggled so hard to read and right
better than all the others. At werst you will have it for a
littel wile and your doing somthing for science.

We are reading a very hard book. Its called *Robinson
Crusoe* about a man who gets merooned on a dessert
Iland. Hes smart and figers out all kinds of things so
he can have a house and food and hes a good swimmer.
Only I feel sorry because hes all alone and has no
frends. But I think their must be somebody else on the
iland because theres a picture with his funny umbrella
looking at footprints. I hope he gets a frend and not
be lonly.

*April* 10    Miss Kinnian teaches me to spell better. She
says look at a word and close your eyes and say it
over and over until you remember. I have lots of truble
with *through* that you say *threw* and *enough* and *tough*
that you dont say *enew and tew*. You got to say *enuff*

and *tuff*. Thats how I use to write it before I started to get smart. Im confused but Miss Kinnian says theres no reason in spelling.

*Apr 14*    Finished *Robinson Crusoe*. I want to find out more about what happens to him but Miss Kinnian says thats all there is. *Why*.

*Apr 15*    Miss Kinnian says Im lerning fast. She read some of the Progress Reports and she looked at me kind of funny. She says Im a fine person and Ill show them all. I asked her why. She said never mind but I shouldnt feel bad if I find out everybody isnt nice like I think. She said for a person who god gave so little to you done more then a lot of people with brains they never even used. I said all my friends are smart people but there good. They like me and they never did anything that wasnt nice. Then she got something in her eye and she had to run out to the ladys room.

*Apr 16*    Today, I lerned, the *comma*, this is a comma (,) a period, with a tail, Miss Kinnian, says its importent, because, it makes writing, better, she said, somebody, coud lose, a lot of money, if a comma, isnt, in the, right place, I dont have, any money, and I dont see, how a comma, keeps you, from losing it,

*Apr 17*    I used the comma wrong. Its punctuation. Miss Kinnian told me to look up long words in the dictionary to lern to spell them. I said whats the difference if you can read it anyway. She said its part of your education so now on Ill look up all the words Im not sure how to spell. It takes a long time to write that way but I only have to look up once and after that I get it right.

You got to mix them up, she showed? me" how. to mix! them (and now; I can! mix up all kinds" of punctuation, in! my writing? There, are lots! of rules? to lern; but Im gettin'g them in my head.

One thing I like about, Dear Miss Kinnian: (thats

the way it goes in a business letter if I ever go into
business) is she, always gives me' a reason" when—I
ask. She's a gen'ius! I wish I cou'd be smart" like, her;
  (Puncuation, is; fun!)


*April* 18   What a dope I am! I didn't even understand what she was talking about. I read the grammar
book last night and it explanes the whole thing. Then
I saw it was the same way as Miss Kinnian was trying
to tell me, but I didn't get it.

Miss Kinnian said that the TV working in my sleep
helped out. She and I reached a plateau. Thats a flat hill.

After I figured out how puncuation worked, I read
over all my old Progress Reports from the beginning. Boy,
did I have crazy spelling and punctuation! I told Miss
Kinnian I ought to go over the pages and fix all the
mistakes but she said, "No, Charlie, Dr. Nemur wants
them just as they are. That's why he let you keep them
after they were photostated, to see your own progress.
You're coming along fast, Charlie."

That made me feel good. After the lesson I went down
and played with Algernon. We don't race any more.


*April* 20   I feel sick inside. Not sick like for a doctor,
but inside my chest it feels empty like getting punched
and a heartburn at the same time. I wasn't going to
write about it, but I guess I got to, because its important. Today was the first time I ever stayed home
from work.

Last night Joe Carp and Frank Reilly invited me to a
party. There were lots of girls and some men from the
factory. I remembered how sick I got last time I drank
too much, so I told Joe I didn't want anything to drink.
He gave me a plain coke instead.

We had a lot of fun for a while. Joe said I should
dance with Ellen and she would teach me the steps. I
fell a few times and I couldn't understand why because
no one else was dancing besides Ellen and me. And all
the time I was tripping because somebody's foot was always sticking out.

Then when I got up I saw the look on Joe's face and it gave me a funny feeling in my stomach. "He's a scream," one of the girls said. Everybody was laughing. "Look at him. He's blushing. Charlie is blushing."

"Hey, Ellen, what'd you do to Charlie? I never saw him act like that before."

I didn't know what to do or where to turn. Everyone was looking at me and laughing and I felt naked. I wanted to hide. I ran outside and I threw up. Then I walked home. It's a funny thing I never knew that Joe and Frank and the others liked to have me around all the time to make fun of me.

Now I know what it means when they say "to pull a Charlie Gordon."

I'm ashamed.

**progress report 11**
*April* 21   Still didn't go into the factory. I told Mrs. Flynn my landlady to call and tell Mr. Donnegan I was sick. Mrs. Flynn looks at me very funny lately like she's scared.

I think it's a good thing about finding out how everybody laughs at me. I thought about it a lot. It's because I'm so dumb and I don't even know when I'm doing something dumb. People think it's funny when a dumb person can't do things the same way they can.

Anyway, now I know I'm getting smarter every day. I know punctuation and I can spell good. I like to look up all the hard words in the dictionary and I remember them. I'm reading a lot now, and Miss Kinnian says I read very fast. Sometimes I even understand what I'm reading about, and it stays in my mind. There are times when I can close my eyes and think of a page and it all comes back like a picture.

Besides history, geography and arithmetic, Miss Kinnian said I should start to learn foreign languages. Dr. Strauss gave me some more tapes to play while I sleep. I still don't understand how that conscious and unconscious mind works, but Dr. Strauss says not to worry yet. He asked me to promise that when I start learning college subjects next week I wouldn't read any books on psychology—that is, until he gives me permission.

I feel a lot better today, but I guess I'm still a little angry that all the time people were laughing and making fun of me because I wasn't so smart. When I become intelligent like Dr. Strauss says, with three times my I.Q. of 68, then maybe I'll be like everyone else and people will like me.

I'm not sure what an I.Q. is. Dr. Nemur said it was something that measured how intelligent you were—like a scale in the drugstore weighs pounds. But Dr. Strauss had a big argument with him and said an I.Q. didn't weigh intelligence at all. He said an I.Q. showed how much intelligence you could get, like the numbers on the outside of a measuring cup. You still had to fill the cup up with stuff.

Then when I asked Burt, who gives me my intelligence tests and works with Algernon, he said that both of them were wrong (only I had to promise not to tell them he said so). Burt says that the I.Q. measures a lot of different things including some of the things you learned already, and it really isn't any good at all.

So I still don't know what I.Q. is except that mine is going to be over 200 soon. I didn't want to say anything, but I don't see how if they don't know *what* it is, or *where* it is—I don't see how they know *how much* of it you've got.

Dr. Nemur says I have to take a *Rorshach Test* tomorrow. I wonder what *that* is.

*April* 22   I found out what a Rorshach is. It's the test I took before the operation—the one with the inkblots on the pieces of cardboard.

I was scared to death of those inkblots. I knew the man was going to ask me to find the pictures and I knew I couldn't. I was thinking to myself, if only there was some way of knowing what kind of pictures were hidden there. Maybe there weren't any pictures at all. Maybe it was just a trick to see if I was dumb enough to look for something that wasn't there. Just thinking about that made me sore at him.

"All right, Charlie," he said, "you've seen these cards before, remember?"

"Of course I remember."

The way I said it, he knew I was angry, and he looked surprised. "Yes, of course. Now I want you to look at this. What might this be? What do you see on this card? People see all sorts of things in these ink-blots. Tell me what it might be for you—what it makes you think of."

I was shocked. That wasn't what I had expected him to say. "You mean there are no pictures hidden in those inkblots?"

He frowned and took off his glasses. "What?"

"Pictures. Hidden in the inkblots. Last time you told me everyone could see them and you wanted me to find them too."

He explained to me that the last time he had used almost the exact same words he was using now. I didn't believe it, and I still have the suspicion that he misled me at the time just for the fun of it. Unless—I don't know any more—could I have been *that* feeble-minded?

We went through the cards slowly. One looked like a pair of bats tugging at something. Another one looked like two men fencing with swords. I imagined all sorts of things. I guess I got carried away. But I didn't trust him any more, and I kept turning them around, even looking on the back to see if there was anything there I was supposed to catch. While he was making his notes, I peeked out of the corner of my eye to read it. But it was all in code that looked like this:

$$WF + A \quad DdF - Ad \text{ orig.} \quad WF - A$$
$$SF + obj$$

The test still doesn't make sense to me. It seems to me that anyone could make up lies about things that they didn't really imagine? Maybe I'll understand it when Dr. Strauss lets me read up on psychology.

*April* 25   I figured out a new way to line up the machines in the factory, and Mr. Donnegan says it will save him ten thousand dollars a year in labor and increased production. He gave me a $25 bonus.

I wanted to take Joe Carp and Frank Reilly out to lunch to celebrate, but Joe said he had to buy some things for his wife, and Frank said he was meeting his cousin for lunch. I guess it'll take a little time for them to get used to the changes in me. Everybody seems to be frightened of me. When I went over to Amos Borg and tapped him, he jumped up in the air.

People don't talk to me much any more or kid around the way they used to. It makes the job kind of lonely.

*April* 27   I got up the nerve today to ask Miss Kinnian to have dinner with me tomorrow night to celebrate my bonus.

At first she wasn't sure it was right, but I asked Dr. Strauss and he said it was okay. Dr. Strauss and Dr. Nemur don't seem to be getting along so well. They're arguing all the time. This evening I heard them shouting. Dr. Nemur was saying that it was *his* experiment and *his* research, and Dr. Strauss shouted back that he contributed just as much, because he found me through Miss Kinnian and he performed the operation. Dr. Strauss said that someday thousands of neuro-surgeons might be using his technique all over the world.

Dr. Nemur wanted to publish the results of the experiment at the end of this month. Dr. Struass wanted to wait a while to be sure. Dr. Strauss said Dr. Nemur was more interested in the Chair of Psychology at Princeton than he was in the experiment. Dr. Nemur said Dr. Strauss was nothing but an opportunist trying to ride to glory on *his* coattails.

When I left afterwards, I found myself trembling. I don't know why for sure, but it was as if I'd seen both men clearly for the first time. I remember hearing Burt say Dr. Nemur had a shrew of a wife who was pushing him all the time to get things published so he could become famous. Burt said that the dream of her life was to have a big shot husband.

*April* 28  I don't understand why I never noticed how beautiful Miss Kinnian really is. She has brown eyes and feathery brown hair that comes to the top of her neck. She's only thirty-four! I think from the beginning I had the feeling that she was an unreachable genius—and very, very old. Now, every time I see her she grows younger and more lovely.

We had dinner and a long talk. When she said I was coming along so fast I'd be leaving her behind, I laughed.

"It's true, Charlie. You're already a better reader than I am. You can read a whole page at a glance while I can take in only a few lines at a time. And you remember every single thing you read. I'm lucky if I can recall the main thoughts and the general meaning."

"I don't feel intelligent. There are so many things I don't understand."

She took out a cigarette and I lit it for her. "You've got to be a *little* patient. You're accomplishing in days and weeks what it takes normal people to do in a lifetime. That's what makes it so amazing. You're like a giant sponge now, soaking things in. Facts, figures, general knowledge. And soon you'll begin to connect them, too. You'll see how different branches of learning are related. There are many levels, Charlie, like steps on a giant ladder that take you up higher and higher to see more and more of the world around you.

"I can see only a little bit of that, Charlie, and I won't go much higher than I am now, but you'll keep climbing up and up, and see more and more, and each step will open new worlds that you never even knew existed." She frowned. "I hope . . . I just hope to God—"

"What?"

"Never mind, Charles. I just hope I wasn't wrong to advise you to go into this in the first place."

I laughed. "How could that be? It worked, didn't it? Even Algernon is still smart."

We sat there silently for a while and I knew what
she was thinking about as she watched me toying with
the chain of my rabbit's foot and my keys. I didn't want
to think of that possibility any more than elderly people
want to think of death. I *knew* that this was only the
beginning. I knew what she meant about levels because
I'd seen some of them already. The thought of leaving
her behind made me sad.

I'm in love with Miss Kinnian.

**progress report 12**

*April* 30 I've quit my job with Donnegan's Plastic
Box Company. Mr. Donnegan insisted it would be better
for all concerned if I left. What did I do to make them
hate me so?

The first I knew of it was when Mr. Donnegan showed
me the petition. Eight hundred names, everyone in the
factory, except Fanny Girden. Scanning the list quickly, I saw at once that hers was the only missing name.
All the rest demanded that I be fired.

Joe Carp and Frank Reilly wouldn't talk to me about
it. No one else would either, except Fanny. She was one
of the few people I'd known who set her mind to something and believed it no matter what the rest of the
world proved, said or did—and Fanny did not believe
that I should have been fired. She had been against the
petition on principle and despite the pressure and threats
she'd held out.

"Which don't mean to say," she remarked, "that I
don't think there's something mighty strange about you,
Charlie. Them changes. I don't know. You used to be a
good, dependable, ordinary man—not too bright maybe,
but honest. Who knows what you done to yourself to
get so smart all of a sudden. Like everybody around
here's been saying, Charlie, it's not right."

"But how can you say that, Fanny? What's wrong
with a man becoming intelligent and wanting to acquire
knowledge and understanding of the world around him?"

She stared down at her work and I turned to leave.
Without looking at me, she said: "It was evil when Eve

listened to the snake and ate from the tree of knowledge. It was evil when she saw that she was naked. If not for that none of us would ever have to grow old and sick, and die."

Once again, now, I have the feeling of shame burning inside me. This intelligence has driven a wedge between me and all the people I once knew and loved. Before, they laughed at me and despised me for my ignorance and dullness; now, they hate me for my knowledge and understanding. What in God's name do they want of me?

They've driven me out of the factory. Now I'm more alone than ever before. . . .

*May 15* Dr. Strauss is very angry at me for not having written any progress reports in two weeks. He's justified because the lab is now paying me a regular salary. I told him I was too busy thinking and reading. When I pointed out that writing was such a slow process that it made me impatient with my poor handwriting, he suggested I learn to type. It's much easier to write now because I can type seventy-five words a minute. Dr. Strauss continually reminds me of the need to speak and write simply so people will be able to understand me.

I'll try to review all the things that happened to me during the last two weeks. Algernon and I were presented to the *American Psychological Association* sitting in convention with the *World Psychological Association.* We created quite a sensation. Dr. Nemur and Dr. Strauss were proud of us.

I suspect that Dr. Nemur, who is sixty—ten years older than Dr. Strauss—finds it necessary to see tangible results of his work. Undoubtedly the result of pressure by Mrs. Nemur.

Contrary to my earlier impressions of him, I realize that Dr. Nemur is not at all a genius. He has a very good mind, but it struggles under the spectre of self-doubt. He wants people to take him for a genius. Therefore it is important for him to feel that his work is accepted by the world. I believe that Dr. Nemur was afraid of further delay because he worried that someone else might make a discovery along these lines and take the credit from him.

Dr. Strauss on the other hand might be called a genius, although I feel his areas of knowledge are too limited. He was educated in the tradition of narrow specialization; the broader aspects of background were neglected far more than necessary—even for a neuro-surgeon.

I was shocked to learn the only ancient languages he could read were Latin, Greek and Hebrew, and that he knows almost nothing of mathematics beyond the elementary levels of the calculus of variations. When he admitted this to me, I found myself almost annoyed. It was as if he'd hidden this part of himself in order to deceive me, pretending—as do many people I've discovered—to be what he is not. No one I've ever known is what he appears to be on the surface.

Dr. Nemur appears to be uncomfortable around me. Sometimes when I try to talk to him, he just looks at me strangely and turns away. I was angry at first when Dr. Strauss told me I was giving Dr. Nemur an inferiority complex. I thought he was mocking me and I'm oversensitive at being made fun of.

How was I to know that a highly respected psychoexperimentalist like Nemur was unacquainted with Hindustani and Chinese? It's absurd when you consider the work that is being done in India and China today in the very field of his study.

I asked Dr. Strauss how Nemur could refute Rahajamati's attack on his method if Nemur couldn't even read them in the first place. That strange look on Strauss' face can mean only one of two things. Either he doesn't want to tell Nemur what they're saying in India, or else —and this worries me—Dr. Strauss doesn't know either. I must be careful to speak and write clearly and simply so people won't laugh.

*May* 18 I am very disturbed. I saw Miss Kinnian last night for the first time in over a week. I tried to avoid all discussions of intellectual concepts and to keep the conversation on a simple, everyday level, but she just stared at me blankly and asked me what I meant about the mathematical variance equivalent in Dorbermann's *Fifth Concerto*.

When I tried to explain she stopped me and laughed. I guess I got angry, but I suspect I'm approaching her on the wrong level. No matter what I try to discuss with her, I am unable to communicate. I must review Vrostadt's equations on *Levels* of *Semantic Progression*. I find I don't communicate with people much any more. Thank God for books and music and things I can think about. I am alone at Mrs. Flynn's boarding house most of the time and seldom speak to anyone.

*May* 20    I would not have noticed the new dishwasher, a boy of about sixteen, at the corner diner where I take my evening meals if not for the incident of the broken dishes.

They crashed to the floor, sending bits of white china under the tables. The boy stood there, dazed and frightened, holding the empty tray in his hand. The catcalls from the customers (the cries of "hey, there go the profits!" . . . *"Mazeltov!"* . . . and "well, *he* didn't work here very long . . ." which invariably seem to follow the breaking of glass or dishware in a public restaurant) all seemed to confuse him.

When the owner came to see what the excitement was about, the boy cowered as if he expected to be struck. "All right! All right, you dope," shouted the owner, "don't just stand there! Get the broom and sweep that mess up. A broom . . . a broom, you idiot! It's in the kitchen!"

The boy saw he was not going to be punished. His frightened expression disappeared and he smiled as he came back with the broom to sweep the floor. A few of the rowdier customers kept up the remarks, amusing themselves at his expense.

"Here, sonny, over here there's a nice piece behind you . . ."

"He's not so dumb. It's easier to break 'em than wash em!"

As his vacant eyes moved across the crowd of on-lookers, he slowly mirrored their smiles and finally broke into an uncertain grin at the joke he obviously did not understand.

I felt sick inside as I looked at his dull, vacuous smile, the wide, bright eyes of a child, uncertain but eager to please. They were laughing at him because he was mentally retarded.

And I had been laughing at him too.

Suddenly I was furious at myself and all those who were smirking at him. I jumped up and shouted, "Shut up! Leave him alone! It's not his fault he can't under-stand! He can't help what he is! But he's still a human being!"

The room grew silent. I cursed myself for losing con-trol. I tried not to look at the boy as I walked out without touching my food. I felt ashamed for both of us.

How strange that people of honest feelings and sensi-bility, who would not take advantage of a man born without arms or eyes—how such people think nothing of abusing a man born with low intelligence. It infuriated me to think that not too long ago I had foolishly played the clown.

And I had almost forgotten.

I'd hidden the picture of the old Charlie Gordon from myself because now that I was intelligent it was some-thing that had to be pushed out of my mind. But today in looking at that boy, for the first time I saw what I had been. *I was just like him!*

Only a short time ago, I learned that people laughed at me. Now I can see that unknowingly I joined with them in laughing at myself. That hurts most of all.

I have often reread my progress reports and seen the illiteracy, the childish naiveté, the mind of low intel-ligence peering from a dark room, through the keyhole at the dazzling light outside. I see that even in my dullness I knew I was inferior, and that other people had something I lacked—something denied me. In my mental blindness, I thought it was somehow connected with the ability to read and write, and I was sure that if I could get those skills I would automatically have intelligence too.

Even a feeble-minded man wants to be like other men.

A child may not know how to feed itself, or what to eat, yet it knows of hunger.

This then is what I was like. I never knew. Even with my gift of intellectual awareness, I never really knew.

This day was good for me. Seeing the past more clearly, I've decided to use my knowledge and skills to work in the field of increasing human intelligence levels. Who is better equipped for this work? Who else has lived in both worlds? These are my people. Let me use my gift to do something for them.

Tomorrow, I will discuss with Dr. Strauss how I can work in this area. I may be able to help him work out the problems of widespread use of the technique which was used on me. I have several good ideas of my own.

There is so much that might be done with this technique. If I could be made into a genius, what about thousands of others like myself? What fantastic levels might be achieved by using this technique on normal people? On *geniuses*?

There are so many doors to open. I am impatient to begin.

**progress report 13**

*May* 23   It happened today. Algernon bit me. I visited the lab to see him as I do occasionally, and when I took him out of his cage, he snapped at my hand. I put him back and watched him for a while. He was unusually disturbed and vicious.

*May* 24   Burt, who is in charge of the experimental animals, tells me that Algernon is changing. He is less co-operative; he refuses to run the maze any more; general motivation has decreased. And he hasn't been eating. Everyone is upset about what this may mean.

*May* 25   They've been feeding Algernon, who now refuses to work the shifting-lock problem. Everyone iden-

tifies me with Algernon. In a way we're both the first
of our kind. They're all pretending that Algernon's behavior is not necessarily significant for me. But it's hard
to hide the fact that some of the other animals who
were used in this experiment are showing strange behavior.

Dr. Strauss and Dr. Nemur have asked me not to
come to the lab any more. I know what they're thinking
but I can't accept it. I am going ahead with my plans
to carry their research forward. With all due respect
to both these fine scientists, I am well aware of their
limitations. If there is an answer, I'll have to find it out
for myself. Suddenly, time has become very important
to me.

*May* 29   I have been given a lab of my own and permission to go ahead with the research. I'm onto something. Working day and night. I've had a cot moved into
the lab. Most of my writing time is spent on the notes
which I keep in a separate folder, but from time to time
I feel it necessary to put down my moods and thoughts
from sheer habit.

I find the *calculus of intelligence* to be a fascinating
study. Here is the place for the application of all the
knowledge I have acquired.

*May* 31   Dr. Strauss thinks I'm working too hard. Dr.
Nemur says I'm trying to cram a lifetime of research
and thought into a few weeks. I know I should rest,
but I'm driven on by something inside that won't let me
stop. I've got to find the reason for the sharp regression
in Algernon. I've got to know *if* and *when* it will happen
to me.

*June 4*

LETTER TO DR. STRAUSS (*copy*)

Dear Dr. Strauss:
    Under separate cover I am sending you a copy of

my report entitled, "The Algernon-Gordon Effect: A Study of Structure and Function of Increased Intelligence," which I would like to have published.

As you see, my experiments are completed. I have included in my report all of my formulae, as well as mathematical analysis in the appendix. Of course, these should be verified.

Because of its importance to both you and Dr. Nemur (and need I say to myself, too?) I have checked and rechecked my results a dozen times in the hope of finding an error. I am sorry to say the results must stand. Yet for the sake of science, I am grateful for the little bit that I here add to the knowledge of the function of the human mind and of the laws governing the artificial increase of human intelligence.

I recall your once saying to me that an experimental *failure* or the *disproving* of a theory was as important to the advancement of learning as a success would be. I know now that this is true. I am sorry, however, that my own contribution to the field must rest upon the ashes of the work of two men I regard so highly.

> Yours truly,
> Charles Gordon

*June 5* I must not become emotional. The facts and the results of my experiments are clear, and the more sensational aspects of my own rapid climb cannot obscure the fact that the tripling of intelligence by the surgical technique developed by Drs. Strauss and Nemur must be viewed as having little or no practical applicability (at the present time) to the increase of human intelligence.

As I review the records and data on Algernon, I see that although he is still in his physical infancy, he has regressed mentally. Motor activity is impaired; there is a general reduction of glandular activity; there is an accelerated loss of coordination.

There are also strong indications of progressive amnesia.

As will be seen by my report, these and other physical and mental deterioration syndromes can be predicted with significant results by the application of my formula.

The surgical stimulus to which we were both subjected has resulted in an intensification and acceleration of all mental processes. The unforeseen development, which I have taken the liberty of calling the *Algernon-Gordon Effect,* is the logical extension of the entire intelligence speed-up. The hypothesis here proven may be described simply in the following terms: Artificially increased intelligence deteriorates at a rate of time directly proportional to the quantity of the increase.

I feel that this, in itself, is an important discovery.

As long as I am able to write, I will continue to record my thoughts in these progress reports. It is one of my few pleasures. However, by all indications, my own mental deterioration will be very rapid.

I have already begun to notice signs of emotional instability and forgetfulness, the first symptoms of the burnout.

*June* 10   Deterioration progressing. I have become absent-minded. Algernon died two days ago. Dissection shows my predictions were right. His brain had decreased in weight and there was a general smoothing out of cerebral convolutions, as well as a deepening and broadening of brain fissures.

I guess the same thing is or will soon be happening to me. Now that it's definite, I don't want it to happen.

I put Algernon's body in a cheese box and buried him in the back yard. I cried.

*June* 15   Dr. Strauss came to see me again. I wouldn't open the door and I told him to go away. I want to be left to myself. I am touchy and irritable. I feel the darkness closing in. It's hard to throw off thoughts of suicide. I keep telling myself how important this journal will be.

It's a strange sensation to pick up a book you enjoyed just a few months ago and discover you don't remember it. I remembered how great I thought John Milton was, but when I picked up *Paradise Lost* I couldn't understand it at all. I got so angry I threw the book across the room.

I've got to try to hold on to some of it. Some of the things I've learned. Oh, God, please don't take it all away.

*June* 19   Sometimes, at night, I go out for a walk. Last night, I couldn't remember where I lived. A policeman took me home. I have the strange feeling that this has all happened to me before—a long time ago. I keep telling myself I'm the only person in the world who can describe what's happening to me.

*June* 21   Why can't I remember? I've got to fight. I lie in bed for days and I don't know who or where I am. Then it all comes back to me in a flash. Fugues of amnesia. Symptoms of senility—second childhood. I can watch them coming on. It's so cruelly logical. I learned so much and so fast. Now my mind is deteriorating rapidly. I won't let it happen. I'll fight it. I can't help thinking of the boy in the restaurant, the blank expression, the silly smile, the people laughing at him. No—please —not that again. . . .

*June* 22   I'm forgetting things that I learned recently. It seems to be following the classic pattern—the last things learned are the first things forgotten. Or is that the pattern? I'd better look it up again. . . .

I re-read my paper on the *Algernon-Gordon Effect* and I get the strange feeling that it was written by someone else. There are parts I don't even understand.

Motor activity impaired. I keep tripping over things, and it becomes increasingly difficult to type.

*June* 23   I've given up using the typewriter. My coordination is bad. I feel I'm moving slower and slower. Had a terrible shock today. I picked up a copy of an article I used in my research, Krueger's *Uber psychische Ganzheit,* to see if it would help me understand what I had done. First I thought there was something wrong with my eyes. Then I realized I could no longer read German. I tested myself in other languages. All gone.

*June* 30 A week since I dared to write again. It's slipping away like sand through my fingers. Most of the books I have are too hard for me now. I get angry with them because I know that I read and understood them just a few weeks ago.

I keep telling myself I must keep writing these reports so that somebody will know what is happening to me. But it gets harder to form the words and remember spellings. I have to look up even simple words in the dictionary now and it makes me impatient with myself.

Dr. Strauss comes around almost every day, but I told him I wouldn't see or speak to anybody. He feels guilty. They all do. But I don't blame anyone. I knew what might happen. But how it hurts.

*July* 7 I don't know where the week went. Todays Sunday I know because I can see through my window people going to church. I think I stayed in bed all week but I remember Mrs. Flynn bringing food to me a few times. I keep saying over and over I've got to do something but then I forget or maybe its just easier not to do what I say I'm going to do.

I think of my mother and father a lot these days. I found a picture of them with me taken at a beach. My father has a big ball under his arm and my mother is holding me by the hand. I dont remember them the way they are in the picture. All I remember is my father drunk most of the time and arguing with mom about money.

He never shaved much and he used to scratch my face when he hugged me. My Mother said he died but Cousin Miltie said he heard his dad say that my father ran away with another woman. When I asked my mother she slapped me and said my father was dead. I dont think I ever found out the truth but I dont care much. (He said he was going to take me to see cows on a farm once but he never did. He never kept his promises. . . .)

*July* 10   My landlady Mrs. Flynn is very worried about me. She says the way I lay around all day and dont do anything I remind her of her son before she threw him out of the house. She said she doesn't like loafers. If Im sick its one thing, but if Im a loafer thats another thing and she won't have it. I told her I think Im sick.

I try to read a little bit every day, mostly stories, but sometimes I have to read the same thing over and over again because I don't know what it means. And its hard to write. I know I should look up all the words in the dictionary but its so hard and Im so tired all the time.

Then I got the idea that I would only use the easy words instead of the long hard ones. That saves time. I put flowers on Algernons grave about once a week. Mrs. Flynn thinks Im crazy to put flowers on a mouses grave but I told her that Algernon was special.

*July* 14   Its sunday again. I dont have anything to do to keep me busy now because my television set is broke and I dont have any money to get it fixed. (I think I lost this months check from the lab. I dont remember)

I get awful headaches and asperin doesnt help me much. Mrs. Flynn knows Im really sick and she feels very sorry for me. Shes a wonderful woman whenever someone is sick.

*July* 22   Mrs. Flynn called a strange doctor to see me. She was afraid I was going to die. I told the doctor I wasnt too sick and I only forget sometimes. He asked me did I have any friends or relatives and I said no I dont have any. I told him I had a friend called Algernon once but he was a mouse and we used to run races together. He looked at me kind of funny like he thought I was crazy. He smiled when I told him I used to be a genius. He talked to me like I was a baby and he winked at Mrs. Flynn. I got mad and chased him out because he was making fun of me the way they all used to.

*July* 24   I have no more money and Mrs Flynn says I got to go to work somewhere and pay the rent because I havent paid for two months. I dont know any work but the job I used to have at Donnegans Box Company. I dont want to go back because they all knew me when I was smart and maybe they'll laugh at me. But I dont know what else to do to get money.

*July* 25   I was looking at some of my old progress reports and its very funny but I cant read what I wrote. I can make out some of the words but they dont make sense.

Miss Kinnian came to the door but I said go away I don't want to see you. She cried and I cried too but I wouldnt let her in because I didn't want her to laugh at me. I told her I didnt like her any more. I told her I didnt want to be smart any more. Thats not true. I still love her and I still want to be smart but I had to say that so shed go away. She gave Mrs. Flynn money to pay the rent. I dont want that. I got to get a job.

Please . . . please let me not forget how to read and write. . . .

*July* 27   Mr. Donnegan was very nice when I came back and asked him for my old job of janitor. First he was very suspicious but I told him what happened to me then he looked very sad and put his hand on my shoulder and said Charlie Gordon you got guts.

Everybody looked at me when I came downstairs and started working in the toilet sweeping it out like I used to. I told myself Charlie if they make fun of you dont get sore because you remember their not so smart as you once thot they were. And besides they were once your friends and if they laughted at you that doesnt meant anything because they liked you too.

One of the new men who came to work there after

I went away made a nasty crack he said hey Charlie I hear your a very smart fella a real quiz kid. Say something intelligent. I felt bad but Joe Carp came over and grabbed him by the shirt and said leave him alone you lousy cracker or I'll break your neck. I didnt expect Joe to take my part so I guess hes really my friend.

Later Frank Reilly came over and said Charlie if anybody bothers you or trys to take advantage you call me or Joe and we will set em straight. I said thanks Frank and I got choked up so I had to turn around and go into the supply room so he wouldnt see me cry. Its good to have friends.


*July* 28  I did a dumb thing today I forgot I wasn't in Miss Kinnians class at the adult center any more like I use to be. I went in and sat down in my old seat in the back of the room and she looked at me funny and she said Charles. I dint remember she ever called me that before only Charlie so I said hello Miss Kinnian Im redy for my lesin today only I lost my reader that we was using. She startid to cry and run out of the room and everybody looked at me and I saw they wasnt the same pepul who use to be in my class.

Then all of a suddin I remembered some things about the operashun and me getting smart and I said holy smoke I reely pulled a Charlie Gordon that time. I went away before she come back to the room.

Thats why Im going away from New York for good. I dont want to do nothing like that agen. I dont want Miss Kinnian to feel sorry for me. Evry body feels sorry at the factery and I dont want that eather so Im going someplace where nobody knows that Charlie Gordon was once a genus and now he cant even reed a book or rite good.

Im taking a cuple of books along and even if I cant reed them Ill practise hard and maybe I wont forget every thing I lerned. If I try reel hard maybe Ill be a littel bit smarter then I was before the operashun. I got my rabits foot and my luky penny and maybe they will help me.

If you ever reed this Miss Kinnian dont be sorry for me Im glad I got a second chanse to be smart becaus I lerned a lot of things that I never even new were in this world and Im grateful that I saw it all for a littel bit. I dont know why Im dumb agen or what I did wrong maybe its because I dint try hard enuff. But if I try and practis very hard maybe Ill get a littl smarter and know what all the words are. I remember a littel bit how nice I had a feeling with the blue book that has the torn cover when I red it. Thats why Im gonna keep trying to get smart so I can have that feeling agen. Its a good feeling to know things and be smart. I wish I had it rite now if I did I would sit down and reed all the time. Anyway I bet Im the first dumb person in the world who ever found out somthing importent for science. I remember I did somthing but I dont remember what. So I gess its like I did it for all the dumb pepul like me.

Goodbye Miss Kinnian and Dr. Strauss and evreybody. And P.S. please tell Dr Nemur not to be such a grouch when pepul laff at him and he would have more frends. Its easy to make frends if you let pepul laff at you. Im going to have lots of frends where I go.

P.P.S. Please if you get a chanse put some flowrs on Algernons grave in the bak yard. . . .

# SO MUCH UNFAIRNESS OF THINGS

## BY C. D. B. BRYAN

The Virginia Preparatory School lies just off the Shirley Highway between Washington, D. C., and Richmond. It is a small Southern school with dull red brick dormitories and classroom buildings, quiet old school buildings with quiet old Southern names—Page House, Stuart Hall, Randolph Hall, Breckinridge, Pinckney, and Coulter. The high brick wall that surrounds the school is known as the Breastworks, and the shallow pond behind the football field is the Crater. V.P.S. is an old school, with an old school's traditions. A sign commemorates the use of the school by Union troops as a military hospital in 1861, and every October the school celebrates "Liberation Day," in honor of the day in 1866 when the school reopened.

Graduates of the Virginia Preparatory School who have not returned for some years are shocked by the glass-and-steel apartment houses and cinder-block ramblers that have sprung up around the school grounds, but once they have driven along the Breastworks and passed through the ornate wrought-iron East Gate, they see, with satisfaction, that the school has not changed. Neither have its customs. For example, new boys, or "toads," still must obey the Toad Code. They must be courteous to old boys and faculty. They must know the school song and cheers by the end of the second week. They must know the names of all members of the faculty and the varsity football team. They must hold doors open for old boys and see that old boys are served first in the dining room. And they must "run relay"—meaning that they have to wake up the old boys in the morning

37

when they wish to be awakened and see that they are not disturbed when they wish to sleep.

Philip Sadler Wilkinson was fourteen; he was an old boy. The new boy shook him lightly. "Mr. Wilkinson? Mr. Wilkinson? It's five-thirty, sir. You asked me to wake you up."

Next year the new boy would be permitted to call Philip Sadler Wilkinson "P.S.," like the others. He watched P.S. stretch, turn over, and go back to sleep. "Sir, hey! Wake up!"

P.S. rolled out of his metal cot, rubbed his eyes, felt around the top of his desk for his glasses, put them on, and looked at the new boy.

"Toad?"

"Yes, sir?"

"What is the date?"

"Thursday, the seventh of June."

"How much longer do we have until the end of the school year?"

"Seven days, twenty-three hours, and"—the new boy looked at his wristwatch—"and thirteen minutes, sir."

P.S. smiled. "Are you sure?"

"No, sir."

"Ah—hah! Ah—HAH! Toad, assume the position!"

The new boy locked his knees and bent over and grabbed his ankles.

"What is a 'toad,' toad?" P.S. asked.

"Sir, a toad is a loathsome warty creature who eats insects and worms, sir. A toad is the lowest form of amphibian. A toad is despicable."

"Well, well, now straighten those knees, toad." P.S. looked at the new boy and saw that his face was turning red with strain. "Toad, are you in pain?"

"No, sir," the new boy lied.

"Then you may straighten up."

The new boy massaged his calves. "Honest to God, P.S., you're a sadist."

"No, no, wait till next year. You'll be pulling the same thing on some toad yourself. I had it done to me, you had it done to you. And did I detect you calling me by my rightful name?"

The new boy smiled.

"Ah, you toads will never learn. Assume the position."

The new boy started to bend over again.

"Oh, go away," P.S. said. The new boy started out of the door and P.S. called him back. "Hey, toad? You gonna kill the Latin exam?"

"I hope so."

"How do you conjugate the verb 'to spit'?"

*"Exspuo, exspuere, exspui—"*

"Heck, no!" P.S. laughed. "It's *spitto, spittere, ach tui, splattus!"*

The new boy ˑgroaned and left the room.


P.S. looked at his watch. It was twenty minutes to six. He could hear the new boy waking up the boy in the next room. P.S. picked up his water glass and toothbrush and tiptoed down the corridor. He stopped at Charlie Merritt's room and knocked softly.

"Who is it?"

"It's me, Charlie."

"Oh, hey, P.S. Come on in."

P.S. pushed aside the curtain of the cubicle. Charlie was sitting at his desk studying.

"Morning," P.S. whispered.

"Morning."

"Studying the Latin?"

"Yep."

"You know how to conjugate the verb 'to spit'?"

"Yep," Charlie said. *"Spitto, spittere, uch—"*

"O.K., O.K.!" P.S. laughed. "You gonna kill the exam?"

"I hope so. You think you'll pass it?"

"Doubt it. I haven't passed one yet." P.S. looked over at Charlie's bureau. "Say, Charlie? Can I borrow your toothpaste? I'm out."

"Sure, but roll it from the bottom of the tube, will you?"

P.S. picked up the toothpaste and went down the hall to the bathroom. Mabrey, the head monitor, was shaving. P.S. watched him in the mirror.

"You must have a porcupine for a father," P.S. said. "You've got the heaviest beard in the school."

Mabrey began to shave the length of his neck. "Wilkinson, you're about as funny as a rubber crutch."

"Cut your throat! Cut your throat!" P.S. began to dance around behind Mabrey, sprinkling voodoo potions on the top of the older student's head. "Monkey dust! Monkey dust! Oh, black Pizoola! Great Kubla of the Ancient Curse! Make this bad man cut his throat!"

Mabrey cursed and a small red stain began to seep through the lather on his throat. "P.S., *will you get out of here!*"

P.S. stared, eyes wide open, at the broadening stain. "Hey! Hey, it worked!"

Mabrey undid the towel from around his waist and snapped P.S.'s skinny behind. P.S. yelped and jumped away. "Hey, Mr. Mabrey, sir? Hey, Mabrey? I'm sorry, I really am. I didn't know it would work."

"What would work?"

"My voodoo curse. I didn't know it would make you cut yourself."

"For Pete's sake, P.S., what're you talking about? I cut a pimple. Will you leave me alone before I throw you out of a closed window?"

P.S. was quiet for a moment. Then he moved over to the washbasin next to Mabrey and looked at himself in the mirror. He ran his fingers through his light-brown hair and pushed his glasses higher on his nose. "Hey, Mabrey? Do you think I'm fresh? I mean, I have great respect for you—you being the head monitor and all. I mean it. Sometimes I worry. I mean, do you think I'm too fresh?"

Mabrey finished rinsing his face. "P.S., kid," he said as he dried himself. "You're all right. You're a nice guy. And I'm willing to bet that if you could only learn to throw a baseball from center field to second base overhand, you might turn out to be a pretty fair little baseball player."

"*Overhand!* Whatddya mean 'overhand'? They call me 'Deadeye Wilkinson'." P.S. wound up with an imaginary baseball and threw it as hard as he could. Then he pantomimed being the second baseman. He crouched and caught the incoming ball at his knees and thrust his hand down to tag out the runner. "*Safe!*" he shouted. "I mean, out! Out! Out!"

"Too late," Mabrey said, and laughed. "An umpire never changes his decision."

"I meant *out*," P.S. said.

Mabrey disappeared down the hall.

P.S. brushed his teeth, being careful to squeeze the toothpaste from the bottom of the tube. He looked at himself in the mirror and chanted, "*Fuero, fueris, fuerit, fuerimus, fueritis, fuerint!*" He examined his upper lip and was disappointed. He wished that he didn't have such a young face. He wished he had a heavy beard, like Mabrey. He washed his face, wet his hair down, and walked back into Charlie's room. Charlie was P.S.'s best friend. He was very short. The other boys kidded him about being an engineer for Lionel trains. P.S. was very tall and thin, and he had not yet grown into his height. At fourteen he was already six feet tall, and he had a tendency to stoop to compensate. He and Charlie were known as Mutt and Jeff. When P.S. entered the room, Charlie was curled up on his bed studying his Latin notes. He didn't look up until P.S. dropped the toothpaste tube on his pillow.

"Rolled from the bottom," P.S. said.

"Hey, how do you expect to pass your Latin exam if you don't study? I heard you and Mabrey clowning around in the can."

"If I don't study!" P.S. said. "Do you know how long I've studied for this exam? If I flunk it again this year, I get to keep the trophy."

"What trophy?"

"For Pete's sake, I don't know what trophy. But I'll get something for sure. I've spent the last two weeks practically doing nothing but studying Latin. I recopied all my notes. I underlined practically the whole book. And I memorized all the irregular verbs. Come on, come on, ask me anything. God, if I don't pass it this year, I've had it. Come on, ask me anything."

"O.K., what's the word for 'ridge'?"

"The word for 'ridge'?" P.S. stalled.

"Yep."

P.S. thought for a moment. "Look, I don't know. Make it two for three."

"The word for 'ridge' is '*iugum*.'" Charlie looked at his notes. "O.K., two out of three. What's the word for 'crowd'? And 'troop,' as in 'a troop of cavalry'?"

"The word for 'crowd' is '*turba, turbae*.' . . . What was the other one?"

" 'Troop of cavalry.' "

" 'Cavalry' is '*equitatus*.' . . . I don't know. What is 'troop'?"

" 'Troop' is '*turma*.' " Charlie laughed. "Well, you got one out of three."

"Did I get partial credit for the 'cavalry'?"

"Nope."

"I hope Dr. Fairfax is more lenient than you are."

"He won't be," Charlie said.

"If I flunk the Latin exam again this year . . ."

"How come you flunked it last year?"

"How come anybody flunks an exam? I didn't know the answers. Boy, Charlie, I don't know what I'm going to do with you. If you weren't such a nice guy and lend me your toothpaste and things like that all the time, I'd probably feed you to the—to the what's-their-name fish. Those fish who eat people in South America all the time."

"Well, since you don't know what to do with me, as a start, why don't you let me study?"

"Sure. Sure, O.K. . . . O.K., be a grind. See if I care."

P.S. walked back to his cubicle and pulled his Ullman

and Henry "Latin II" from his unpainted bookcase. First he studied the irregular verbs in the back of the book. Then he went over his vocabulary list. He concentrated for as long as he could; then he leaned out of his window to look at the shadows of the trees directly below, dropped a penny out of the window to see if a squirrel would pick it up, checked his window sill to see if the cookie crumbs he had left for the mockingbird were still there.

He turned back to his Latin book and leafed through the Forestier illustrations of Roman soldiers. He picked up the picture his father had given him last Christmas. Within the frame were four small round photographs of Wilkinsons in uniform. There was his father as an infantry major during the Second World War, his grandfather as a captain in the field artillery during the First World War, his great-great-grandfather as a corporal in a soft gray Confederate uniform and a great-great-great-great something or other in a dark uniform with a lot of bright buttons. P.S. didn't know who the last picture was of. He imagined it to be somebody from the Revolutionary War. P.S. had seen the oil portrait the photograph had been taken from hanging in the hallway of his grandfather's house. P.S. had the long, thin nose of the other Wilkinsons in the pictures, but he still had the round cheeks of youth and the perfect eyebrows. He was the fifteenth of his family to attend the Virginia Preparatory School. Among the buildings at V.P.S. there was a Wilkinson Memorial Library and a Sadler Gymnasium. When P.S. was packing to begin his first year at the school, his father had said, "Son, when your great-grandfather went off to V.P.S., his father gave him a dozen silk handkerchiefs and a pair of warm gloves. When I went off to V.P.S., your grandfather gave me a dozen silk handkerchiefs and a pair of warm gloves. And now here are a dozen silk handkerchiefs and a pair of warm gloves for you."

P.S. looked at the brightly patterned Liberty-silk handkerchiefs and the fuzzy red mittens. No thirteen-year-old ever wore red mittens, except girls, and particularly not fuzzy red mittens. And P.S. knew he would never dare to wear the silk handkerchiefs.

"Well, thank you very much, Dad," he said.

"That's all right, son."

P.S. left the red mittens behind when he went away to V.P.S. He used two of the silk handkerchiefs to cover the top of his bureau and bookcase, gave one other away to a girl, and hid the rest beneath his underwear on the second shelf of his bureau. His father had done very well at the school; he had been a senior monitor, editor-in-chief of the yearbook, and a distance runner in winter and spring track. P.S. hoped he would do as well, but he knew he had disappointed his father so far. When he flunked the Latin examination last year and tried to explain to his father that he just could not do Latin, he could see the disbelief in his father's eyes. "Good Lord, son, you just didn't study. 'Can't do Latin,' what nonsense!" But P.S. knew that studying had nothing to do with it. His father said that no Wilkinson had ever flunked at V.P.S.; P.S. was the first. His father was not the kind to lose his temper. P.S. wished he were. When P.S. had done something wrong, his father would just look at him and smile sadly and shake his head.

The boy had never felt particularly close to his father. He had never been able to talk to or with his father. He had found the best means of getting along with his father was to keep out of his way. He had given up their ever sharing anything. He had no illusions about leading a calendar-picture life with his father—canoeing or hunting together. He could remember trying to get his father to play catch with him and how his father would always say, "Not now, son, not now." But there were certain occasions that his father felt should be shared with P.S. These were the proper father-son occasions that made P.S. feel like some sort of ornament. There would be Father's Day, or the big football game of the season. P.S. would be told to order two tickets, and the afternoon of the game he and his father would watch the first half together. His father remembered all of the

cheers and was shocked when P.S. didn't remember some
of the words to the school song. At the half, his father
would disappear to talk to his friends and P.S. would
be left alone to watch the overcoats or umbrellas.

After the game P.S. would wander back to the field
house, where the alumni tables were set up. He would
locate his father and stand next to him until his father introduced him to the persons he was talking to. Then his
father would say, "Run along, son. I'll meet you back in
your room." So, P.S. would go back to his room and
wait for his father to come by. The boy would straighten
up the bed, dust the bureau, and sweep the floor. And
then after a long wait his father would come in and sit
down. "Well, how are you, son?" the conversation would
always start. And P.S. would answer, "Fine, thank you,
sir." His father would look around the room and remark
about its not being large enough to swing a cat in, then
there would be two or three anecdotes about the times
when he was a boy at V.P.S., and then he would look at
his watch and say, "Well, I guess I'd better be pushing
off." His father would ask him if there was anything he
needed, and P.S. would say that he didn't think there
was anything. His father would give him a five-dollar
bill and drive away. And P.S., with enormous relief,
would go look for Charlie. "Did you and your dad have
a good time?" Charlie would ask. "Sure," P.S. would say.
And that would end the conversation.

P.S. knew that his father loved him, but he also knew
better than to expect any sign of affection. Affection always seemed to embarrass his father. P.S. remembered
his first year at school, when his father had first come
up to see him. He had been very happy to see his father,
and when they were saying goodbye P.S. stepped forward as usual to kiss him and his father drew away. P.S.
always made it a point now to shake hands with his
father. And at fourteen respect and obedience had taken
the place of love.

P.S. picked up his Latin notes and went over the translations he had completed. He wished he knew what ques-

tions would be asked. In last year's exam there were questions from all over the book, and it made the exam very difficult to study for, if they were going to do that. He pictured himself handing in the finished examination to Dr. Fairfax and saying, "Sir? Wilkinsons do not flunk. Please grade my exam accordingly."

P.S. looked at his wristwatch. The dining hall would begin serving breakfast in fifteen minutes. He made his bed and put on a clean pair of khakis and a button-down shirt. He slipped into his old white bucks and broke a lace tying them, and pulled out the shorter piece and threaded what was left through the next eyelet up, as the older boys did. He tidied up his room for inspection, picked up his notes, and went back to Charlie's room. Charlie was sweeping the halls and emptying all trash baskets. P.S. entered and sat down on the bed.

"Hey, P.S.! I just made the bed!"

"O.K., O.K., I'll straighten it up when I leave." P.S. ran his fingers across the desk top. "Merritt, two demerits—dust. . . . Hey, you know what, Charlie?"

Charlie dusted the desk and then said, "What?"

"You're such a grump in the morning. I sure'd hate to be married to you."

"Well, I wouldn't worry about that. In the first place, my parents wouldn't approve."

"I'm not so sure that my family would want me to marry a Merritt, either. I think you'd have to take my family name. I mean, you know, you're just not our class."

"P.S., buddy, you're in a class all by yourself."

"Well, anyway, what I mean is that you're such a grump in the morning that I can see someday your wife coming in—if you ever find a girl who's foolish enough to marry you. But I mean, she might come in some morning and give you grapefruit juice instead of orange juice and you'll probably bite her hand off or something."

"Or *something*." Charlie laughed.

P.S. punched Charlie on the arm. "Garbage mind!"

"What do you mean? I didn't say anything. You've

got the dirty mind. All I said was 'or something' and you say I've got a garbage mind."

"Well, you know what I meant."

"I don't know anything at all."

P.S. looked at Charlie for a moment, then he laughed. "I'm not going to take advantage of your last remark. I'm much too good a sport to rake you over the coals when you place your ample foot in your ample mouth."

"*Ample foot!*" Charlie held up his foot. "I've got a very small foot. It's a sign of good breeding."

"Only in horses, Twinkletoes, only in horses."

"Horses, *horses!* What do horses have to do with it?"

"Ask me no questions and I'll tell you no lies." P.S. leafed through Charlie's notes. "Hey, the exam's at ten-thirty, isn't it?"

"Yep. If you flunk Latin again, will they make you go to summer school?"

"Probably. I really think it's archaic the way they make you pass Latin to get out of this place."

"Boy, I sure hope I pass it," Charlie said.

"You will. You will. You're the brain in the class."

"Come on, let's go to chow."

"That's what I've been waiting for, my good buddy, my good friend, old pal of mine." P.S. jumped off the bed, scooped up his notebook, and started out of the room.

"Hey!" Charlie said. "What about the bed?"

At eight o'clock chapel, P.S. knelt in the pew and prayed: "*Dear God, I pray that I pass my Latin exam this morning. . . . If I can pass this exam, then I'll do anything you want me to do. . . . God, please. If I don't pass this exam, I've really had it. . . . They must have made these pews for midgets; I never fit in them right. . . . How am I ever going to get out to Colorado this summer unless I pass that exam? . . . Please God, I don't want a high grade, all I want is to pass . . . and you don't have to help me on the others. . . . I don't want to pass this exam for myself only. I mean, it means a lot to my family. My father will be very disappointed*

*if I flunk the exam.* . . . I wonder if Charlie will be able
to go out to Colorado with me. . . . *God bless Mom,
God bless Dad, God bless Grandpa Sadler and Grandma
Sadler, God bless Grandpa Wilkinson and Granny
Wilkinson, God bless all my relatives I haven't mentioned . . . Amen. And . . . and God? Please, please
help me to pass this exam."*

At ten-fifteen, P.S. and Charlie fell in step and walked
over to Randolph Hall, where the examination was to
be held.

"Well, if we don't know it now, we never will," Charlie
said.

"Even if I did know it now, I wouldn't know it tomorrow." P.S. reached into his pants pocket and pulled out
his lucky exam tie. It was a stained and unraveled blue
knit. As they walked up the path, he was careful to tie
the tie backward, the wide end next to his shirt, the seam
facing out. Then he checked his watch pocket to see
that his lucky silver dollar was there.

"What's the Latin for 'then'?" Charlie asked.

" *'Tum,'* " P.S. answered. "Tums for your *tummy.*"

"What's the word for 'thence,' or 'from there'?"

*"Inde."* P.S. began to sing: *"Inde* evening byde
moonlight you could *hearde*—"

"For Pete's sake, P.S.!" Charlie laughed.

"You don't like my singing?"

"Not much."

"You know? I'm thinking of joining the choir and glee
club next year. You know why? They've got a couple of
dances next fall. One with St. Catharine's and another
with St. Tim's. You wanta try out with me?"

"I don't know. I can't sing."

"Who's gonna sing?" P.S. grabbed Charlie's arm and
growled, "Baby, I'm no singer, I'm a lover!"

"Lover? Who says you're a lover?"

"Ask me no question and I'll tell you no lies."


P.S. and Charlie walked up the worn wooden steps of
Randolph Hall to the third-floor study hall, where the
Latin examination was to be given. They both were in

the upper study hall, since they were underclassmen still. P.S.'s desk was in the back corner of the study hall, against the wall. He sat down and brushed the dust off the top of his desk with his palm. Someone had traced a hand into the wood. Others had traced and retraced the hand and deepened the grooves. They had added fingernails and rings. P.S. had added a Marlboro tattoo. He lifted the desk top and, searching for his pencil sharpener, saw that he had some more Latin translations in his desk. He read them through quickly and decided it was too late to learn anything from them. He pulled out his pencil sharpener and closed his desk. The study hall was filling with boys, who took their places at their desks and called back and forth to each other in their slow Southern voices. It was a long, thin room with high windows on either side, and the walls were painted a dirty yellow. Between the windows were framed engravings of Roman ruins and Southern generals. The large fluorescent lights above the desks buzzed and blinked into life. A dark, curly-haired boy sat down in the desk next to P.S. and began to empty his pockets of pencils and pens.

"Hey, Jumbo," P.S. said. "You gonna kill the exam?"

"I hope so. If I can get a good grade on it, then I don't have to worry so much about my math exam tomorrow."

"Well, if we don't know it now we never will."

"You're right."

Jumbo had played second-string tackle on the varsity this year. He was expected to be first-string next year, and by his final year, the coaches thought, he might become an All-Virginia High School tackle. Jumbo was a sincere, not very bright student who came from a farm in Virginia and wanted to be a farmer when he finished college. P.S. had sat next to Jumbo all year, but they had never become particularly close friends. Jumbo lived in a different dormitory and had a tendency to stick with the other members of the football team. But P.S. liked him, and Jumbo was really the only member of the football team that he knew at all.

P.S. looked up at the engraving of General Robert E. Lee and his horse, Traveller. He glanced over at Jumbo. Jumbo was cleaning his fingernails with the tip of his automatic pencil.

"Well, good luck," P.S. said.

"Good luck to you."

"I'll need it."

P.S. stood up and looked for Charlie. "Hey! Hey, Charlie?"

Charlie turned around. "Yeah?"

*"Piggo, piggere, squeely, gruntum!"*

"For Pete's sake, P.S.!"

"Hey, P.S.?" someone shouted. "You gonna flunk it again this year?"

"No, no, I don't think so," P.S. answered in mock seriousness. "In point of fact, as the good Dr. Fairfax would say—in point of fact, I might just come out with the highest grade in class. After all, I'm such a brain."

The noise in the study hall suddenly stopped; Dr. Fairfax had entered. The Latin instructor walked to the back of the study hall, where P.S. was sitting.

"And what was all that about, Wilkinson?"

"Sir, I was telling the others how I'm the brain in your class."

"Indeed?" Dr. Fairfax asked.

"Yes, sir. But I was only kidding."

"Indeed," the Latin instructor said, and the other students laughed.

Dr. Fairfax was a large man with a lean, aesthetic face, which he tried to hide with a military mustache. He had taught at the Virginia Preparatory School since 1919. P.S.'s father had had Dr. Fairfax for a Latin instructor. When P.S. read "Goodbye, Mr. Chips," he had kept thinking of Dr. Fairfax. The Latin instructor wore the same suit and vest all winter. They were always immaculate. The first day of spring was marked by Dr. Fairfax's appearance in a white linen suit, which he always wore with a small blue bachelor's-button. Before a study hall last spring, someone had placed an alarm clock set to go off during the middle of study hall in one of the tall wastepaper baskets at the rear of the room. The student had then emptied all of the pencil sharpeners and several ink bottles into the basket and covered all this with crumpled-up pad paper. When the alarm clock went off, Dr. Fairfax strode down the aisle and reached into the wastepaper basket for the clock. When he lifted it out, the sleeve of his white linen jacket was covered with ink and pencil shavings. There was a stunned silence in the study hall as Dr. Fairfax looked at his sleeve. And then Dr. Fairfax began to laugh. The old man sat down on one of the desk tops and laughed and laughed, until finally the students had enough nerve to join him. The next day, he appeared in the same linen suit, but it was absolutely clean. Nobody was given demerits or punished in any manner. Dr. Fairfax was P.S.'s favorite instructor. P.S. watched him separate the examination papers and blue books into neat piles at the proctor's desk. Dr. Fairfax looked up at the electric clock over the study-hall door and then at his thin gold pocket watch. He cleared his throat. "Good morning, gentlemen."

"GOOD MORNING, SIR!" the students shouted.

"Gentlemen, there will be no talking during the examination. In the two hours given you, you will have ample time to complete all of the necessary work. When the bell sounds signifying the end of examination, you will cease work immediately. In point of fact, anyone found working after the bell will be looked upon most unfavorably. When you receive your examinations, make certain that the print is legible. Make sure that you place your names on each of your blue books. If you have any difficulty reading the examination, hold your hand above your head and you will be given a fresh copy. The tops of your desks should be cleared of all notes, papers and books. Are there any questions? . . . If not, will Baylor and you, Grandy, and . . . and Merritt . . . will the three of you please pass out the examinations."

P.S. watched Charlie get up and walk over to the desk. Dr. Fairfax reached into his breast pocket and pulled out a pair of steel-rimmed spectacles. He looked out across the room. "We are nearing the end of the school year," he said. "Examinations always seem to cause students an undue amount of concern. I assure you, I can well remember when I was a student at V.P.S. In point of fact, I was not so very different from some of you—"

The instructor was interrupted by a rasping Bronx cheer. He looked quickly over in the direction of the sound. "Travers, was that you?"

"No, sir."

"Brandon, was that you?"

The student hesitated, then answered, "Yes, sir."

"Brandon, I consider that marked disrespect, and it will cost you ten demerits."

"Aww, sir—"

"Fifteen." Dr. Fairfax cleared his throat again. "Now, if I may continue? . . . Good. There are a few important things to remember when taking an examination. First, do not get upset when you cannot at once answer all of the questions. The examination is designed—"

P.S. stopped listening. Charlie was walking down the aisle toward him.

"Hey, Charlie," he whispered, "give me an easy one."

"There will be no favoritism on my part."

"How does it look?"

"Tough."

"Merritt and Wilkinson?" Dr. Fairfax said. "That last little bit of conversation will cost you each five demerits."

The Latin instructor looked up at the electric clock again. "When you receive your examinations, you may begin. Are there any questions? . . . If not, gentlemen, it might be well for us to remember this ancient Latin proverb: '*Abusus non tollit usum.*'" Dr. Fairfax waited for the laugh. There was none. He cleared his throat again. "Perhaps . . . perhaps we had better ask the class brain what the proverb means. Wilkinson?"

P.S. stood up. "'*Abusus non tollit usum,*' sir?"

"That's right."

"Something like '*Abuse does not tolerate the use,*' sir?"

"What does the verb '*tollo, tollere, sustuli, sublatus*' mean?"

"To take away, sir."

"That's right. The proverb, then, is 'Abuse does not take away the use,' or, in the context I was referring to, just because you gentlemen cannot do Latin properly does not mean that it should not be done at all."

"Yes, sir," P.S. said, and he sat down.

Dr. Fairfax unfolded his newspaper, and P.S. began to read the examination. He picked up his pencil and printed in large letters on the cover of his blue book:

PHILIP SADLER WILKINSON

LATIN EXAMINATION

LATIN II—DR. FAIRFAX

VIRGINIA PREPARATORY SCHOOL

7 JUNE 1962—BOOK ONE (1)

Then he put down his pencil, stretched, and began to work.

P.S. read the examination carefully. He saw that he would be able to do very little of it from memory, and felt the first surge of panic moisten his palms. He tried to translate the first Latin-to-English passage. He remembered that it fell on the right-hand side of the page in his Ullman and Henry, opposite the picture of the Roman galley. The picture was a still taken from the silent movie version of "Ben-Hur." He recognized some of the verbs, more of the nouns, and finally he began to be able to translate. It was about the Veneti ships, which were more efficient than the Roman galleys because they had prows and flat keels. He translated the entire passage, put down his pencil, and stretched again.

An hour later, P.S. knew he was in trouble. The first translation and the vocabulary section were the only parts of the exam he had been able to do without too much difficulty. He was able to give the rule and examples for the datives of agent and possession. The English-to-Latin sentences were the most difficult. He had been able to do only one of those. For the question "How do you determine the tense of the infinitive in indirect

statement?" he wrote, "You can determine the tense by
the construction of the sentence and by the word end-
ings," and hoped he might get some credit. The two
Latin-to-English passages counted twenty points apiece.
If he could only do that second translation, he stood a
chance of passing the examination. He recognized the
adverb *"inde,"* but he saw that it didn't help him very
much. The examination was halfway over. He tried to
count how many points he had made so far on the
examination. He thought he might have somewhere between fifty and fifty-five. Passing was seventy. If he could
just translate that second passage, he would have the
points he needed to pass. Dr. Fairfax never scaled the
grades. P.S. had heard that one year the Latin instructor
flunked everybody but two.

He glanced over at Jumbo. Then he looked back down
at his own examination and swore under his breath.
Jumbo looked over at him and smiled. P.S. pantomimed
that he could not answer the question, and Jumbo smiled
again. P.S. slid his glasses off and rubbed his eyes. He
fought down the panic, wiped his hands on his pants legs,
and looked at the passage again. He couldn't make any
sense out of the blur of the words. He squinted, looked
at them, put on his glasses again, and knew that he was
in trouble.

He leaned over his desk and closed his eyes. *Dear God,
please help me on this examination . . . please, God,
please . . . I must pass this examination. . . .* He opened
his eyes and looked carefully around to see if anyone
had seen him praying. The others were all working hard
on the examination. P.S. looked up again at the engraving on the wall above his desk. Beneath the portrait was
the caption "Soon after the close of the War Between
the States, General Robert E. Lee became the head of a
school for young men. General Lee made this statement
when he met with his students for the first time: 'We
have but one rule in this school, and that is that every
student must be a gentleman.' " They left out that other
rule, P.S. thought. They left out the one that says you

have to have Latin to graduate! Or is that part of being a gentleman, too?

He read the Latin-to-English passage through twice, then he read it through backwards. He knew he had seen the passage before. He even remembered seeing it recently. But where? He knew that the passage dealt with the difficulties the Romans were having in fortifying their positions, but there were so many technical words in it that he could not get more than five of the twenty points from the translation, and he needed at least fifteen to pass. . . . He was going to flunk. *But I can't flunk! I can't flunk! I've got to pass!*

P.S. knew if he flunked he wouldn't be able to face his father. No matter what excuse P.S. gave, his father would not believe he hadn't loafed all term.

He looked at the passage and tried to remember where he had seen it. And then his mouth went dry. He felt the flush burn into the back of his neck and spread to his cheeks. He swallowed hard. *The translation's in my desk! . . . It's in my desk! . . . oh, Lord! . . . It's the translation on the top of the stack in my desk . . . in my desk!*

All he would have to do would be to slip the translation out of his desk, copy it, put it away, and he would pass the examination. All of his worries would be over. His father would be happy that he passed the examination. He wouldn't have to go to summer school. He and Charlie could go out to Colorado together to work on that dude ranch. He would be through with Latin forever. The Latin grade would never pull his average down again. Everything would be all right. Everything would be fine. All he would have to do would be to copy that one paragraph. Everyone cheated. Maybe not at V.P.S. But in other schools they bragged about it. . . . Everyone cheated in one way or another. Why should that one passage ruin everything? Who cared what problems the Romans had!

P.S. glanced over at Jumbo. Jumbo was chewing on

his pencil eraser as he worked on the examination. Dr. Fairfax was still reading his newspaper. P.S. felt his heart beat faster. It began beating so hard that he was certain Jumbo could hear it. P.S. gently raised his desk top and pretended to feel around for a pencil. He let his blue book slide halfway off his desk so it leaned in his lap. Then he slid the translation under the blue book and slid the blue book and notes back onto his desk. He was certain that everyone had seen him—that everyone knew he was about to cheat. He slowly raised his eyes to look at Dr. Fairfax, who went on reading. P.S. covered part of the notes with his examination and began to copy the rest into his blue book. He could feel the heat in his cheeks, the dryness in his mouth. *Dear God . . . God, please don't let them catch me! . . . Please!*

He changed the smooth translation into a rough one as he copied, so that it would match his other translation.

*From these things the army was taught the nature of the place and how the slope of the hill and the necessity of the time demanded more than one plan and order for the art of war. Different legions, some in one part, others in another, fought the enemy. And the view was obstructed by very thick hedges. Sure support could not be placed, nor could it be seen what work would be necessary in which part, nor could all the commands be administered by one man. Therefore, against so much unfairness of things, various consequences ensued.*

He put down his pencil and looked around the study hall. No one was watching. P.S. carefully slid the translation back into his desk. He looked to see if the translation gave him any words that might help him on the rest of the examination. His heart was still beating wildly in his chest, and his hands shook. He licked his lips and concentrated on behaving normally. *It's over. . . . It's over. . . . I've cheated, but it's all over and no one said anything!*

He began to relax.

Fifteen minutes later, Dr. Fairfax stood up at his desk, looked at the electric clock, then down at his pocket watch. He cleared his throat and said, "Stop!"

Several students groaned. The rest gathered up their pencils and pens.

"Make certain you have written out the pledge in full and signed it," Dr. Fairfax said.

P.S. felt the physical pain of fear again. He opened his blue book and wrote, "I pledge on my honor as a gentleman that I have neither given nor received unauthorized assistance on this examination." He hesitated; then he signed his name.

"Place your examination inside your blue book," Dr. Fairfax continued. "Make certain that you put your name on your blue book. . . . Baylor? If you and, uh, Ferguson and Showalter will be good enough to pick up the examinations, the rest of you may go. And, um, gentlemen, your grades will be posted on the front door of my office no sooner than forty-eight hours from now. In point of fact, any attempt to solicit your grade any sooner than that will result in bad temper on my part and greater severity in the marking of papers. Are there any questions? . . . If not, gentlemen, dismissed."

The students stood up and stretched. An immediate, excited hum of voices filled the study hall. P.S. looked down at his exam paper. He slid it into his blue book and left it on his desk.

Charlie was waiting at the door of the study hall. "Well, P.S., how'd the brain do?"

"You know it's bad luck to talk about an exam before the grades are posted."

"I know. I'm just asking how you think you did."

"I don't know," P.S. said.

"Well, well, I mean, do you think you passed?"

"*I don't know!*"

"Whooey!" Charlie whistled. "And you called *me* a grump!"

They walked down the stairs together. At the bottom,

Charlie asked P.S. if he was going to go to lunch. "No, I don't think so," P.S. said. "I'm not feeling so well. I think I'll lie down for a while. I'll see ya."

"Sure," Charlie said. "See ya."

In his cubicle in Memorial Hall, P.S. took off his lucky exam tie. He put his silver dollar back onto his bookcase. He reached inside the hollow copy of *Gulliver's Travels* for the pack of cigarettes he kept there. Then he walked down the corridor to the bathroom, stepped into one of the stalls and locked the door. He lit the cigarette and leaned his forehead against the cool green marble divider. He was sick with fear and dread. *It's over! It's all over!* he said, trying to calm himself. He did not like the new knowledge he had of himself. He was a cheater. He rolled his forehead back and forth against the stone, pressing his forehead into it, hurting himself. P.S. had broken the Honor Code of the school, and he was scared.

*I shouldn't have cheated! What if someone had seen me! I shouldn't have cheated! Maybe somebody did see me. . . . Maybe Dr. Fairfax will know I cheated when he sees my exam. . . . Maybe somebody will check my desk after the exam and find the copy of the translation. . . . I cheated. Damn it, I cheated! Stupid, damned fool. . . . What if somebody finds out! . . . Maybe I should turn myself in. . . . I wonder if they'd kick me out if I turned myself in. . . . It would prove that I really am honest, I just made a mistake, that's all. . . . I'll tell them I couldn't help it. . . . Maybe they'll just give me a reprimand.*

But P.S. knew that if he turned himself in, they would tell his parents he had cheated, so what good would that do? His father would be just as angry. Even more so, since Wilkinsons don't cheat, either. P.S. knew how ashamed his father would make him feel. His father would have to tell others that P.S. had cheated. It was a part of the Southern tradition. "My son has disgraced me. It is better that you hear it from me than some-

body else." His father would do something like that. And
having other people know he had cheated would be too
much shame to bear. And even if he did turn himself
in, the school would make him take another exam. . . .
And he'd flunk that one, too. . . . He knew it. . . .
*Oh, God, what am I going to do?*

If he didn't turn himself in and no one had seen him,
then who would know? He would never cheat again. If
he could just get away with it this one time. Then everything would be O.K. Nobody need ever know—except
himself. And P.S. knew he would never be able to forget that he had cheated. Maybe if he turned himself in,
it would be better in the long run. *What long run? What
the hell kind of long run will I have if I turn myself
in? Everybody in the school will know I cheated, no
matter whether I turn myself in or not. . . . They won't
remember me for turning myself in. . . . They'll remember that I cheated in the first place. . . .*

P.S. wanted to cry, but he couldn't. He dropped the
cigarette into the toilet and flushed it down. Then he
went over to the sink and rinsed his mouth out. He
had some chewing gum in his room; that would cover
the smell of his smoking. He looked at himself in the
mirror. He couldn't see any change since this morning,
and yet he felt so different. He looked at his eyes to see
if there were lines under them now. *What shall I do?*
he asked his reflection. *What the hell shall I do?* He
turned on the cold water and rinsed his face. He dried
himself on a towel someone had left behind, and walked
back down the corridor to his room. He brushed aside
the curtain, entered the cubicle, and stopped frozen with
fear. Mabrey, the head monitor, was sitting on P.S.'s
bed.

"Wilkinson," Mabrey said, "would you mind coming
with me? Just outside for a few minutes."

"What about?"

Mabrey got up from the bed. "Come on, P.S."

"What . . . What do you want me for?"

"We want to talk to you."

*We!* WE! P.S. picked up his jacket and started to put it on.

"You won't need your jacket," Mabrey said, as he walked into the corridor.

"It doesn't matter, I'll wear it anyway."

P.S. followed Mabrey out of the dormitory. *I didn't have a chance to turn myself in,* he thought. *I didn't have a chance to choose. . . .*

"You think you'll make the varsity baseball team next year?" Mabrey asked.

"I don't know," P.S. said. *What is he talking about baseball for?*

The new boy who had wakened P.S. passed them on the walk. He said hello to both Mabrey and P.S. He received no answer and shrugged.

Mabrey and P.S. took the path to the headmaster's office. P.S. could feel the enormous weight of the fear building up inside him again. Mabrey opened the door for P.S. and ushered him into the headmaster's waiting room. Nelson, a pale, fat-faced senior, was sitting there alone. He was the secretary of the Honor Committee. P.S. had always hated him. The other members of the Honor Committee were Mabrey, the vice-president; Linus Hendricks, the president; Mr. Seaton, the headmaster; and Dr. Fairfax, who served as faculty adviser. Mabrey motioned that P.S. was to sit down in the chair facing the others—the only straight-backed wooden chair in the room. Every now and then, Nelson would look up at P.S. and shake his head. The door to the headmaster's office opened and Mr. Seaton came out, followed by Linus Hendricks, Dr. Fairfax, and—*Lord, what is Jumbo doing here! Don't tell me he cheated, too! He was sitting right next to me!* Jumbo walked out of the room without looking at P.S.

Linus Hendricks waited for the others to seat themselves, then he sat down himself and faced P.S. "Well, P.S., I imagine you know why you're here."

P.S. looked at Hendricks. Hendricks was the captain

of the football team. He and Mabrey were the two most important undergraduates in the school.

"Well, P.S.?" Hendricks repeated.

"Yes, sir," P.S. said.

He could feel them all staring at him. He looked down at his hands folded in his lap. He could see clearly every line in his thumb knuckle. He could see the dirt caught under the corner of his fingernail, and the small blue vein running across the knuckle.

He looked up at Dr. Fairfax. He wanted to tell him not to worry. He wanted to tell him that he was sorry, so very sorry.

The headmaster, Mr. Seaton, was a young man. He had just become the headmaster of V.P.S. this year. He liked the students, and the students liked him. He was prematurely bald, and smiled a lot. He had a very young and pretty wife, and some of the students were in love with her and fought to sit at her table in the dining room. Mr. Seaton liked to play tennis. He would play the students and bet his dessert that he would win. And most of the time he would lose, and the students were enormously pleased to see the headmaster of the school have to get up from the table and pay his bets. Mr. Seaton would walk very quickly across the dining hall, his bald head bent to hide his smile. He would swoop up to a table, drop the dessert—and depart, like a bombing airplane, P.S. could tell that the headmaster was distressed he had cheated.

Linus Hendricks crossed his legs and sank back into the deep leather armchair. Mabrey and Nelson leaned forward as though they were going to charge P.S.

"P.S.," Hendricks said. "You're here this afternoon because the Honor Committee has reason to suspect that you may have cheated on the Latin exam this morning. We must ask you whether or not this is true."

P.S. raised his head and looked at Hendricks. Hendricks was wearing a bright striped tie. P.S. concentrated on the stripes. Thick black, thin white, medium green, thin white, and thick black.

"P.S., did you, or did you not, cheat on the Latin examination?"

P.S. nodded.

"Yes or no, P.S.?" Hendricks asked.

P.S. no longer felt anything. He was numb with misery. "Yes," he said, in a small, tired voice. "Yes, I cheated on the examination. But I was going to turn myself in. I was going to turn myself in, I swear I was."

"If you were going to turn yourself in, why didn't you?" Nelson asked.

"I couldn't . . . I couldn't yet. . . ." P.S. looked at Dr. Fairfax. "I'm sorry, sir. I'm terribly sorry. . . ." P.S. began to cry. "I'm so ashamed. . . . Oh, God. . . ." P.S. tried to stop crying. He couldn't. The tears stung his eyes. One tear slipped into the inside of his glasses and puddled across the bottom of the lens. He reached into his back pocket for a handkerchief, but he had forgotten to bring one. He started to pull out his shirt-tail, and decided he'd better not. He wiped his face with the side of his hand.

Mr. Seaton walked over to P.S. and gave him his hand-kerchief. The headmaster rested his hand on P.S.'s shoulder. "Why, P.S.? Why did you cheat?"

P.S. couldn't answer.

"P.S., you were the last boy I expected this of. Why did you feel you had to cheat on this exam?"

"I don't know, sir."

"But P.S., you must have had some reason."

Nelson said, "Answer the headmaster when he's asking you a question, Wilkinson."

P.S. looked up at him with such loathing that Nelson looked away.

Mr. Seaton crouched down next to P.S. "You must have been aware of the penalty for cheating."

P.S. nodded.

"Then why, in heaven's name, did you risk expulsion to pass the examination?"

"Sir—sir, I flunked Latin last year, sir. I knew I'd flunk it this year, too. I—I knew I couldn't pass the Latin exam ever."

"But why did you *cheat*?"

"Because . . . because, sir, I had to pass the exam."

The headmaster ran his hand across his forehead. "P.S., I'm not trying to trick you, I'm only trying to understand why you did this thing. Why did you bring the notes into the exam with you?"

"Sir, Mr. Seaton, I didn't bring the notes in, they were in my desk. If they hadn't been, I wouldn't be here. I didn't want to cheat. I didn't *mean* to cheat. I—it was just the only way I could pass the exam."

Nelson rested his pudgy arms on the sides of his leather armchair and looked at the headmaster and then back to P.S. Then he said, "Wilkinson, you have been in V.P.S. for two years. You must be familiar, I imagine, with the Honor Code. In fact, in your study hall there is a small wooden plaque above the proctor's desk. On it are carved the four points of the Honor Code: 'I will not lie. I will not steal. I will not cheat. I will report anyone I see doing so.' You are familiar with them, aren't you?"

"Of course I'm familiar with them," P.S. said impatiently.

"Why did you think you were so much better than everyone else that you could ignore it?"

"I don't think I'm better than everyone else, Nelson," P.S. said.

"Well, you sure aren't! The others don't cheat." Nelson sat back again, very satisfied with himself.

Dr. Fairfax came from behind the chairs and stood next to P.S. "Unless you hold your tongue, Nelson— unless you hold your tongue, I shall personally escort you out of here."

"But, sir," Nelson whined. "I'm only trying to—"

"SHUT UP!" Dr. Fairfax roared. He returned to the back of the room.

Mr. Seaton spoke again. "P.S., if you had flunked this exam, you would have been able to take another. Perhaps you would have passed the re-examination. Most boys do."

"I wouldn't have, sir," P.S. said. "I just cannot do
Latin. You could have given me fifty examinations, sir.
And I don't mean any disrespect, but I would have
flunked all fifty of them."

Mabrey asked the headmaster if he could speak. Then
he turned to P.S. "P.S., we—all of us have been tempted
at some time or another to cheat. All of us have either
resisted the temptation or, perhaps, we were lucky enough
to get away with it. I think that what we want to know
is what *made* you cheat. Just having to pass the exam
isn't enough. I know you, P.S. I may know you better
than anyone in the room, because I've shared the same
floor in the dorm with you for this year. And we were
on the same floor when you were a toad. You're not
the kind who cheats unless he has a damn good—"
Mabrey glanced over at the headmaster. "Excuse me, sir.
I didn't mean to swear."

The headmaster nodded and indicated that Mabrey
was to continue.

"What I mean is this, P.S. I know you don't care
how high your grade is, just so long as you keep out of
trouble. . . . You're one of the most popular boys in
your class. Everybody likes you. Why would you throw
all of this over, just to pass a Latin exam?"

"I don't know. I don't know. . . . I had to pass the
exam. If I flunked it again, my father would kill me."

"What do you mean he would 'kill' you?" Mr. Seaton
asked.

"Oh, nothing, sir. I mean—I don't mean he would
hurt me. He would just—Oh, I don't know how to explain it to you. If I flunked the exam again, he'd just
make me feel so, I don't know . . . *ashamed* . . . so
terrible. I just couldn't take it again."

There was a moment of silence in the room. P.S.
began to cry again. He could tell the headmaster still
didn't understand why he had cheated. He looked down
at his hands again. With his index finger he traced
the veins that crossed the back of his hand. He looked
over at the wooden arm of his straight-backed chair. He

could see the little drops of moisture where his hand had squeezed the arm of the chair. He could make out every grain of wood, every worn spot. He took off his glasses and rubbed his eyes. He tried taking deep breaths, but each time his breath would be choked off.

Hendricks cleared his throat and recrossed his legs. "P.S.," he said, "we have your examination here. You signed your name to the pledge at the end of the exam. You swore on your honor that you had not cheated." Hendricks paused. P.S. knew what he was driving at.

"If I hadn't signed my name to the pledge, you would have known I had cheated right away," P.S. explained. "I didn't want to break my honor again. I was going to turn myself in, honest I was."

"You didn't, though," Nelson said.

"I would have!" P.S. said. But he still wasn't sure whether he would have or not. He knew he never would be certain.

"So, we've got you on lying and cheating," Nelson said. "How do we know you haven't stolen, too?"

Dr. Fairfax grabbed the lapels of Nelson's jacket, pulled him out of the chair, and pushed him out of the room. The old man closed the door and leaned against it. He wiped his brow and said, "Mr. Seaton, sir, I trust you won't find fault with my actions. That young Nelson has a tendency to bother me. In point of fact, he irritates me intensely."

P.S. looked gratefully at Dr. Fairfax. The old man smiled sadly. Mabrey was talking quietly to Hendricks. Mr. Seaton sat down in Nelson's chair and turned to P.S. "I know this is a difficult question. Would you—would you have turned Jumbo in had you seen him cheating?"

P.S. felt the blood drain from his face. *So Jumbo turned me in! . . . Jumbo saw me! . . . Sitting next to me all year! . . . Jumbo turned me in! Why?*

He looked up at the others. They were all waiting for his answer. He had the most curious feeling of aloofness, of coldness. If he said yes, that he would have turned

Jumbo in, it would be a lie, and he knew it. If he answered yes, it would please the headmaster, though. Because it would mean that P.S. still had faith in the school system. If he said no, he wouldn't have turned Jumbo in, it would be as good as admitting that he would not obey the fourth part of the Honor Code—"I will report anyone I see doing so." He waited a moment and then answered, "I don't know. I don't know whether I would have turned Jumbo in or not."

"Thank you very much, P.S.," the headmaster said.

P.S. could tell that Mr. Seaton was disappointed in his answer.

"Gentlemen, do you have any further questions you would like to ask Wilkinson?"

"Nothing, sir," Hendricks answered.

The headmaster looked over at Dr. Fairfax, who shook his head. "Well, then, P.S., if you don't mind, we'd like you to sit in my office until we call for you."

P.S. got up and started for the door.

"Have you had any lunch?" Dr. Fairfax asked.

"No, sir. But I'm not very hungry."

"I'll have Mrs. Burdick bring in some milk and cookies."

"Thank you, sir."


The door opened and P.S. stood up as Mr. Seaton walked over to his desk and eased himself into the swivel chair. P.S. had been sitting alone in the headmaster's office for several hours.

"Sit down, please," the headmaster said. He picked up a wooden pencil and began to roll it back and forth between his palms. P.S. could hear the click of the pencil as it rolled across the headmaster's ring. Mr. Seaton laid the pencil aside and rubbed his cheek. His hand moved up the side of his face and began to massage his temples. Then he looked up at P.S. and said, "The Honor Committee has decided that you must leave the school. The penalty for cheating at V.P.S. is immediate expulsion. There cannot be any exceptions."

P.S. took a deep breath and pushed himself back into

the soft leather seat. Then he dropped his hands into his lap and slumped. He was beyond crying; there was nothing left to cry about.

"Your father is waiting for you in the other room," Mr. Seaton said. "I've asked him to wait outside for a few minutes, because I want to speak to you alone. I want you to understand why the school had to make the decision to expel you. The school—this school—is only as good as its honor system. And the honor system is only as good as the students who live by it."

P.S. cleared his throat and looked down at his fingernails. He wished the headmaster wouldn't talk about it. He knew why the school had to expel him. It was done. It was over with. What good would it do to talk about it?

"The honor system, since it is based on mutual trust and confidence, no doubt makes it easier for some students to cheat," the headmaster said. "I am not so naïve as to believe that there aren't any boys who cheat here. Unfortunately, our honor system makes it easy for them to do so. These boys have not been caught. Perhaps they will never be caught. But I feel that it was far better for you to have been caught right away, P.S., because you are not a cheater. Notice that I said you *are* not a cheater instead of you *were* not a cheater. . . . Yes, you cheated this one time. I do not need to ask whether you cheated before. I know you haven't. I know also that you will not cheat again. I was frankly stunned when I heard that you had cheated on Dr. Fairfax's examination. You were the last boy I would have expected to cheat. I am still not entirely satisfied by the reasons you gave for cheating. I suppose a person never is. Maybe it is impossible to give reasons for such an act." Mr. Seaton began massaging his temple again. "P.S., the most difficult thing that you must try to understand is that Jumbo did the right thing. Jumbo was correct in turning you in."

P.S. stiffened in the chair. "Yes, sir," he said.

"If no one reported infractions, we would have no Honor Code. The Code would be obeyed only when it was convenient to obey it. It would be given lip service. The whole system would break down. The school would become just another private school, instead of the respected and loved institution it now is. Put yourself in Jumbo's shoes for a moment. You and Jumbo are friends —*believe me,* you are friends. If you had heard what Jumbo said about you in here, and how it hurt him to turn you in, you would know what a good friend Jumbo is. You have been expelled for cheating. You will not be here next fall. But Jumbo will be. Jumbo will stay on at V.P.S., and the other students will know that he was the one who turned you in. When I asked you whether you would have turned Jumbo in, you said that you didn't know. You and I both know from your answer that you wouldn't have turned Jumbo in. Perhaps the schoolboy code is still stronger in you than the Honor Code. Many students feel stronger about the schoolboy code than the Honor Code. No one likes to turn in a friend. A lot of boys who don't know any better, a lot of your friends, will never forgive Jumbo. It will be plenty tough for him. Just as it is tough on anybody who does his duty. I think—I honestly think that Jumbo has done you a favor. I'm not going to suggest that you be grateful to him. Not yet. That would be as ridiculous as my saying something as trite as 'Someday you will be able to look back on this and laugh.' . . . P.S., you will *never* be able to look back on this and laugh. But you may be able to understand." The headmaster looked at his wristwatch and then said, "I'm going to leave you alone with your father for a few minutes; then I suggest you go back to your room and pack. The other students won't be back in the dormitories yet, so you can be alone." He got up from behind the desk. P.S. rose also. He looked down at the milk and cookies Mrs. Burdick had left him. There was half a glass of milk and three cookies left.

The headmaster looked at P.S. for a moment and then he said, "I'm sorry you have been expelled, P.S. You were a good student here. One of the most popular boys in your class. You will leave behind a great many good friends."

"Thank you, sir," P.S. said.

"I'll see you before you and your father leave."

"Yes, sir."

The headmaster walked into the waiting room. P.S. could hear Dr. Fairfax talking, and then his father. The door closed, and P.S. sat down to wait for his father. He could feel the fear building up inside of him again. He did not know what to say to his father. What could he say? He sipped the last of the milk as the door opened. P.S. put down the glass and stood up.

Stewart Wilkinson closed the door behind him and looked at his son. He wanted to hold the boy and comfort him, but Phil looked so solid, so strong, standing there. Why isn't he crying, he wondered, and then he told himself that he wouldn't have cried, either; that the boy had plenty of time to cry; he would never cry in front of his father again. He tried to think of something to say. He knew that he often was clumsy in his relations with Phil, and said the wrong thing, and he wondered whether he had been that sensitive at his son's age. He looked down at the plate of cookies and the empty milk glass.

"Where did you get the milk and cookies, son?"

"Mrs. Burdick brought them to me, sir."

He never calls me "Dad" now, Stewart Wilkinson said to himself. Always "sir." . . . My own son calls me "sir." . . .

"Did you thank her?"

"Yes, sir."

Stewart Wilkinson walked over to the couch next to his son and sat down. The boy remained standing.

"Phil, son, sit down, please."

"Yes, sir."

Looking at his son, Stewart Wilkinson could not understand why they had grown apart during the last few years. He had always remained close to his father. Why wasn't it the same between him and the boy who sat so stiff beside him, so still in spite of the horror he must have gone through during the past few hours?

"I'm sorry, sir."

"Yes . . . yes, son, I know you are. . . . I'm terribly sorry myself. Sorry for you. . . . Mr. Seaton told me another boy turned you in, is that right?"

P.S. nodded.

"He also told me that he believes you would have turned yourself in had you been given enough time."

"I don't know whether I would have or not. I never had a chance to find out."

"I think you would have. I think you would have."

He waited for his son to say something; then, realizing there was nothing the boy could say, he spoke again. "I was talking to Dr. Fairfax outside—you knew he was my Latin teacher, too?"

"Yes, sir."

"We always used to be able to tell when the first day of spring came, because Dr. Fairfax put on his white linen suit."

"Yes, sir."

"At any rate, that man thinks very highly of you, Phil. He is very upset that you had to be expelled. I hope you will speak to him before we go. He's a good man to have on your side."

"I want to speak to him."

"Phil . . . Phil . . ." Stewart Wilkinson thought for a minute. He wanted so desperately what he said to be the right thing to say. "Phil, I know that I am partly responsible for what has happened. I must have in some way pressured you into it. I wanted your marks to be high. I wanted you to get the best education that you could. V.P.S. isn't the best school in the country, but it's a damn fine one. It's a school that has meant a lot to our family. But that doesn't matter so much. I mean, that part of it is all over with. I'm sorry that you cheated, because I know you're not the cheating kind. I'm also sorry because you are going to have to face the family and get it over with. This is going to be tough. But they'll all understand. I doubt that there is any of us who have never cheated in one way or another. But it will make them very proud of you if you can go see them and look them in the eye."

He picked up one of the cookies and began to bite little pieces out of the edge. Then he shook his head sadly, in the gesture P.S. knew so well. "Ah, son, it's so terrible that you have to learn these lessons when you are young. I know that you don't want me to feel sorry for you, but I can't help it. I'm not angry with you. I'm a little disappointed, perhaps, but I can understand it, I think. I suppose I must appear as an ogre to you at times. But Phil, I—If I'm tough with you, it's just because I'm trying to help you. Maybe I'm too tough." Stewart Wilkinson looked over at his son. He saw that the boy was watching him. He felt a little embarrassed to have revealed so much of himself before his son. But he knew they were alike. He knew that Phil was really his son. They already spoke alike. Already laughed at the same sort of things, appreciated the same things. Their tastes were pretty much the same. He knew that, if anything, he was too much like the boy to be able to help him. And also that the problem was the boy's own, and that he would resent his father's interfering.

"Phil, I'll go speak with Mr. Seaton for a little while, and then I'll come on over and help you pack. If you'd like, I'll pack for you and you can sit in the car."

"No, that's all right, sir, I'll pack. I mean, most of the stuff is packed up already. I'll meet you over there."

Stewart Wilkinson rose with his son. Again he wanted to hold the boy, to show him how much he loved him.

"I'll be through packing in a few minutes. I'll meet you in my room," P.S. said.

"Fine, son."

Together they carried the footlocker down the staircase of Memorial Hall. P.S. stopped at the door, balanced the footlocker with one hand, then pulled the heavy door

open. The door swung back before they could get
through. Stewart Wilkinson stumbled and P.S. said, "I'm
sorry."

They carried the footlocker across the small patch
of lawn between the front of Memorial Hall and the
main drive and slid the footlocker into the back of the
station wagon.

"How much more is there, son?"

"A couple of small boxes, some books, and a couple
of pictures."

Stewart Wilkinson pulled a silk handkerchief out of
his back pocket and wiped his brow. "You think we
can get all of them in one more trip?"

"I think so, sir. At least, we can try."

They turned back toward the dormitory. Stewart
Wilkinson rested his hand on his son's shoulder as they
walked back across the lawn. "Phil, Mr. Seaton told me
that he thinks he might be able to get you into Hotchkiss.
How does that sound to you?"

"It's a funny name for a school."

"Hotchkiss, funny? Why?"

"I don't know, it just sounds funny."

"Well, do you think you'd like to go there?"

"Sure. I mean I don't know. I haven't given it much
thought."

Stewart Wilkinson laughed. "I guess you haven't."

The boy looked worriedly at his father for a moment.
He wondered whether his father was making fun of him.
And then he saw the humor in his remark and laughed,
too.

They brought the last of the boxes down from the
room and slid them into the car and closed the tailgate.

"Did you get a chance to talk to Dr. Fairfax?"

"Yes, sir. He came by the room while I was packing."

"What did he say?"

"I don't know. I mean he was sorry I was going and
all that, but he said I'd get along fine anywhere and
that it wasn't the end of the world."

"Did he say 'in point of fact'?"

"Yeah." P.S. laughed. "He said, 'Well, boy, you'll do all right. In point of fact, you have nothing to worry about.' I really like old Doc Fairfax."

They went around the side of the car and climbed in.

"Anything you've forgotten? Books out of the library, equipment in the gym? Anybody special you want to see before we go home?"

"No, Dad, thanks, that's all—Hey, wait a minute, could you, Dad?" P.S. got out of the car. "It's Charlie —Charlie Merritt. I'd like to say goodbye to him."

"Sure, son, take your time."

The two boys spoke together for a moment, standing in the road; then they shook hands. Stewart Wilkinson turned off the engine and watched as the boys walked back to the road toward him. As they drew near, he got out of the station wagon.

"Dad, this is Charlie Merritt. . . . Charlie, you remember my father."

"Yes, sir. How are you, sir?"

"Fine, thank you, Charlie."

"Sir, Mr. Wilkinson, I'm sorry about P.S. getting kicked out and all."

Stewart Wilkinson nodded.

"He's just sorry because I won't be around to borrow his toothpaste any more. He likes to lend it to me because I always roll it from the top and lose the cap."

P.S. and Charlie laughed.

"Hey, P.S.?" Charlie said. "Does this mean you're not going to have to work off the five demerits Doc Fairfax gave us this morning?"

"What did you two get five demerits for?" Stewart Wilkinson asked.

"We were talking about the exam," P.S. said.

Father and son looked at each other, and then P.S. turned away. It was clear that he was thinking about the exam and his cheating again. And then the boy took a deep breath and smiled. "You know? It's funny," he said. "I mean, it seems that exam took place so long ago. . . . Well, Charlie." P.S. stuck out his hand and

Charlie took it. "Well, I guess we'd better get going. I'll see you around, O.K.?"

"Sure, P.S.," Charlie said.

The two boys shook hands again solemnly. Then Charlie shook hands with P.S.'s father. P.S. and Stewart Wilkinson got back into the station wagon.

Charlie walked around to P.S.'s window. "Hey, P.S.? Make sure you let me hear from you this summer, O.K.?"

"Sure, Charlie. Take care of yourself."

They drove around the school drive, by the Wilkinson Memorial Library and the Sadler Gymnasium and then they turned down the slight hill toward the Breastworks, and as they passed through the ornate, wrought-iron gate P.S. began to cry.

# BACKWARD BOY

BY GENE COGHLAN

When I smell spruce smoke I smell a great slice of my past; I smell Alaska and a little cluster of log buildings at the edge of a small lake sandwiched between the Wasilla Woods and the foothills of the Talkeetna Mountains. And I see only too painfully, too nostalgically clear, the first group of pupils I taught in Alaska —thirty-six motley, eager young faces representing eight grades.

And I see "Auber." The head of bushy black hair surmounted an enormous pair of limpid brown eyes. His small thin body clad in blue jeans and patched plaid shirt of threadbare cotton seemed scarcely adequate support for that great mass of hair and eyes.

It seems incredible after all these years that the pupil hardest to forget was the dumbest I ever taught. He couldn't even pronounce his own name on his first day at school.

"Say it again, please," I said. "I'm afraid I didn't hear it quite right."

"Auber," he said again. "Auber Dubois."

"He means *Albert,* teacher!" shrilly proclaimed a somewhat bigger boy who, I soon learned, was Auber's brother, Marcel, known to everybody as Junior.

I had gone north to teach—and with some half-formed hopes of finding a husband, although at the time I wasn't admitting the latter even to myself. I was the first teacher in the log school in Bulldozer, a village that owed its existence to a stampede of World War II veterans in quest of a brave new world. Where there'd been only the scattered cabins of trappers, prospectors

75

and fishermen, there had sprung into being a complete
community.

There were a store and a post office—both in the
same building—and Paulson's sawmill, a great open-
sided shed with a flat roof and huge piles of lumber
and slabs. There were the log church and the new log
school. The school was off to one side in a clearing of
its own on a flat woody bench overlooking a small oval-
shaped lake.

My school was so new, in fact, that the freshly peeled
spruce logs still gleamed whitely against the brown and
yellow of the autumn birch leaves. My living quarters
were to be in two rooms above the classroom. I had a
wood-burning cookstove, a table and two chairs, a small
built-in cupboard, a badly bruised davenport—and the
lower half of an Army double-decker wooden bunk.

On the short opening day of school little is ever ac-
complished in the way of education. The teacher seats
the pupils and tries to maintain order while she starts
down the front row and up the next with necessary questions: What is your name? How old are you? What
grade are you in?

Then discipline can be relaxed and the teacher—if she
is conscientious—tries to work it out so that in spite of
the age differences the entire classroom melts into one
unit. I felt lucky in achieving just this kind of rapport on
my first day at Bulldozer School. In fact, everything
came off so incredibly well that when I announced early
dismissal nobody wanted to leave.

One boy, a twelve-year-old native, told me that he
wanted to stay but couldn't because he had to go and
help his father "quarter-up" and pack out a moose they
had killed that morning. I had never experienced anything like this! A warm feeling came over me, and I
was at a loss what to say. So I asked the contentedly
babbling faces about another odd thing I had noticed:
"Don't any parents ever accompany beginners to school
on the first day in Alaska?"

The clamor of answering voices rose to such a crescendo I had to signal for silence by waving my hand, palm forward, back and forth several times. At last I singled out a girl in blue jeans and blouse and said, "Would you please explain, miss?"

"Sure," she said quickly. "It's potato harvest and everybody's working."

"Your mothers too?" I asked.

"Of course, and we'd all have to pick spuds too if we went home now. That's why we want to stay in school."

All this time I was conscious of Auber's tremendous brown eyes glued to my face. He wasn't saying anything, but he certainly was taking it all in. His thick hair was unkempt and uncombed, long at the back and long at the temples where it tapered off to a point about midway down the ear.

"It is too nice a day to stay indoors," I announced. "We will go out and sit on the grassy bank and look across the lake at the beautiful scenery while we get better acquainted." This brought quite a gust of laughter, for they thought I must be joking.

Auber's brother spoke up, "We don't see nothing but scenery all our lives. This is the first school me and Auber ever been in and we like it. Our daddies built it and some of us bigger kids helped peel the logs." Junior was eight.

"How can this be your first school when some of you are in the eighth grade?" I asked.

"That's just the homesteader kids," Junior explained. "They all went to school 'outside.' Me an' Auber and some of the other kids never saw the inside of a real school. My mamma taught me. We don't even know what grade I'm in."

In the face of all the unprecedented enthusiasm for school I just couldn't coldly dismiss these children, not even after lunch—and all had brought lunches. I let them stay the full seven hours.

As it turned out, Junior was one of my brightest pupils. Auber was my slowest. A good teacher is supposed to be objective and impartial. I don't think many succeed. But Auber was the only pupil I ever openly favored, and he was the only teacher's pet I ever knew of who was gladly accepted as such by the other pupils—as though he were their pet too.

Auber, though small and thin, was tough as whang leather and active as a chickadee. Slow in scholastic things, he was quick in other ways. Right from the beginning, when there were bigger and stronger boys in the room, he took care of the huge stove—a converted 100-gallon gasoline drum. Only rarely did he need help to get a big log in far enough so he could close the stove door.

When I passed out the report cards on the last day of school in the spring, there were three "retainees"— educators' euphemism for "flunkers." I couldn't take my gaze from Auber, who had extracted his report card from the envelope and now held it opened before him. I knew he couldn't read "Failed," which I had written in longhand with a note for his parents that read: "I feel very badly about this. But it wouldn't be fair to the other first-graders if I passed Auber."

Auber looked toward Junior two rows away. When Junior finally glanced toward Auber and saw him holding the report card he said, "Teacher? May I speak to Auber?"

"Why, certainly, Junior. Didn't I say that you could all talk as long as you didn't yell?"

"But you didn't say we could leave our desks, and if I speak to Auber from here I will have to holler."

"You are right," I said. "You may leave your seat."

Now the other pupils were listening. By the time Junior reached Auber's desk it was dead quiet in the school.

"You didn't pass, Auber," Junior said. "You will be in the first grade again next year." It was the clap of doom.

For a moment Auber merely looked startled. He was even a slow learner of bad news. Then the great innocent eyes went shiny and the tiny triangle of face made a gallant effort to conceal heartbreak. The dam broke and Auber's tears came in a deluge.

Junior Dubois placed his arm across Auber's shoulders as the sobs shook the little frame.

"You may move around and talk while I go upstairs and put some potatoes on to boil," I said. I had to fight to keep from bolting for the staircase against the west wall. The children were used to my quick trips to attend to my cooking and thought nothing of this one.

I burst into tears and flung myself on my cot with my face in my pillow. I couldn't shake Auber's stricken look and I wished I could just die. It took a good half hour to "put those potatoes on to boil."

The glow a teacher gets from watching a gifted student work can never compensate for the sadness when a "slow" child is denied promotion.

Albert Dubois became a project. I wanted to teach him so badly that I fear there were times when I was guilty of slackening off on the rest of the pupils. It just didn't seem possible that such a sensitive child, so kind and gentle and understanding, could really and truly be "dumb." I sought desperately for a chink in that delicate little psyche through which I might probe and inject some knowledge.

I also had to keep Auber two years in the fourth grade. By then he had learned some control; he also was able to read the word "Failed" without help from Junior. This time the brave little face won the battle of the tear ducts, and only the additional shininess in the big, tender brown eyes showed that the hurt was there. Auber exhibited a mild spurt his second year in the fourth grade. I couldn't have been more overjoyed if he had been my own son. *Now,* I hastily concluded, *my efforts are telling. Soon Auber's potentially fine brain will break its chains and he will catch up—maybe even pass the children he started to school with.* There were now only four of the latter, all in the sixth grade—an average group.

I redoubled my efforts. Auber had always been better than average at drawing, for he was a born observer.

A teacher with eight grades, alas, has no time for an art
class, no time for soap sculpture, no time for square
dancing and no time for socializing. But here was one
teacher who found time for one student's art. I know
little of art myself, but I encouraged Auber to draw,
draw, draw. His drawing never improved beyond the
point his little spurt took it. The spurt also brought improvement in composition and enough improvement in
other subjects to justify my passing Auber. But in looking back I am afraid I rationalized a little.

I was simply so gone on him that I could not bear
again the terrific emotional punishment of denying him
his promotion.

Nevertheless, at the end of seventh grade I had to break
the boy's heart for the third time. If only he could
have been a nasty pupil or a dumb brute of a child;
but Auber, if anything, had become unbelievably good.
He was my janitor, my fireman, my wood-packer-upper
(upstairs to my living quarters) and my water boy. He
had grown considerably, and the lower part of his face
was now catching up with his eyes. His father kept
that hair cut shorter, and Auber now occasionally used
a comb.

When Auber began his second year in the seventh
grade, Junior was starting his second year of high school
at Wasilla, a bus run having been arranged by the Bulldozer community. Auber's sister, Grace, was in fifth
grade while another sister, Marie, was in second. These
other Dubois children were all above-average pupils.

One gray day in early November I sat correcting
compositions at my desk in the poorly lighted classroom. The first one, written by a girl, read, "My mother
was learning to drive the truck and she ran clean over
the meat house daddy had just bilt." She never mentioned what daddy said. Then came the usual hodge-
podge of dull or, at best, mediocre writing. The last
composition, however, was a distinct surprise.

Auber had written it! His grammar and spelling were
as discouraging as ever, which means he was at fourth-

grade level or worse; but he wrote in a bold and legible hand.

Maybe I cry too easily; it just seems that everything of any importance that ever happened to Auber was tied to my tear ducts.

One cold day pa come faling along the trale. Me and Junior was diging in the snow for wood but it was all gone. Pas nose was wite and we new it was froze. Me and Junior sneked in the back dore wile pa fel in the front. Wen he stagered to the stoave and leand agen it Ma slamed the front dore shut that pa had left open and said HUG THAT STOAVE CLOSE YOU DRUNKERD. THE FIRES BEN OUT FOR HOURS [Auber used capitals for the quotation marks he never understood] Then pa slid to the flore and ma threw the comfiter over him. The girls were scaired and big eyed in the corner. We was all cold in bed that night but pa who slept the best. Pa sure can stand the cold.

Mrs. Stroup, whose husband trucked supplies to Bulldozer and hauled lumber to Anchorage, had once said to me, "Marcel Dubois tries hard in that simple way of his; but between you and me I think he could drink less and feed his family more." Then again, the father of one of my pupils, Jack Herkimer, had said, "Marcel is a trapper, and furs aren't worth anything. In the summer he is a salmon fisherman in Cook Inlet, and the salmon in Cook Inlet are nearly gone. They say Marcel drinks too much. I don't think he drinks a damn bit more than the rest of us; only they notice him more because they know he can't afford it. Anyway, that wife of his never lets him forget that she is educated, while he barely learned to read and write."

I was so pleased with Auber's graphic description of Marcel Dubois' drunken home-coming that I slipped the seventh-graders another composition assignment before the customary lapse of one week was up. I didn't dare praise Auber, although I wanted to in the worst way. I was so afraid a wrong move might throw Auber's creativity out of gear. Whereas I usually assigned the topic and made the pupils build their writing around it, this time I turned them loose to write about subjects of their own choosing.

Auber did it again. It wasn't much, only a short paragraph; still, if I could keep that little spark alive, maybe I could fan it into a full-blown flame.

Our home was quite. You could hear a snowflake drop. Then down the stares fel my sister Marie. Ma she screamed and run to the bottom of the stares and said OH MY POOR BABY. Of course Marie was four then wich is a big baby any time. DON'T TUTCH HER pa yeled YOU WILL RUNE HER SPINE. Wile my fokes yeled at eatch other Marie she clumb the stares agen and fel right back down on purposs. She liked the atentson that mutch. She got a licken this time. It was a exiting day.

I saw Marcel Dubois in the store one day. I cornered him back in the little post office at the end of the dry-goods counter. "Marcel," I said, "Auber is beginning to write stories. Maybe you could quietly encourage him at home."

"Now, Lizbet," Marcel replied (he could never pronounce "Elizabeth"). "Please, I know Auber is slow. I know you try hard. He will soon be out of school. That is enough. I will teach him w'at I know—trapping, hunting, woodcutting; only I don't know about trapping because Auber say it is cruel. He lak the garden, but even so he say, 'The vegetable hurt too w'en you pull him, papa.'" Marcel looked at me with Auber's clear brown eyes. He had the same thick black hair. But where Auber was small and thin, his father was of medium height and heavy-set and strong. He had big hands and thick fingers. But he was known to be extremely generous and kindly—when he was sober, that is.

After we broke off our conversation and were standing in line for our mail at the general-delivery counter, Marcel said, "Auber will be sixteen in February. Then he can leave shool."

It made me mad. I snapped, "You dumb old Frenchie; you just let Auber finish out the year. If you break that boy's heart, I will——" I didn't know what to say next. Marcel flashed his strong white teeth in a big grin and said, "Boy! Is me tough!"

Auber's creativity continued on a somewhat lighter note.

One day wen I come home from school Mrs. Fogerty stood behind ma who sat in a chare with her hare all flatened down and her head all nobby bumps. The house smelled awfle. YOU NEEDN'T TURN UP YOUR NOSE Mrs. Fogerty said YOUR MOTHER IS GETTING A PURMINNINT. The next day ma looked the prittiest we ever seen her. Her hare was fluffy and curley and brown. She looked a lot in the mear that day and she sang a lot. When pa come home with a load of wood in the truk he come in the house and said OH WHAT A BEUTY I GOT FOR A BRIDE. Ma blushed and us kids all laughed and claped our hands. She said to pa OH YOU DONT MEAN IT.

Truly I was riding on a cloud. All my years of trying to help an unfortunate pupil were at last bearing fruit. I continually had to force myself to remember that there were other pupils in my room too. With fingers crossed I read Auber's latest. It must have represented a Herculean effort on his part. It was written in two paragraphs!

My father had no job one fall and all him and ma chewd the rag about was how broke we was. The moose meat was gone and Frosty our dog was thin. He was a big husky and could pul three of us at one time on the sled.

Christmas morning wen we got up there was preasants for all of us kids. I got a air rifle and Junior he
got shoe packs and the girls got dolls. But we had
only a rabit for dinner for us all and some boiled
potatose. Then Junior he said WARE IS FROSTY.
We couldnt find him and the girls and Junior cride.
I felt bad to but I didnt want them to see me cry
so I went and cride outside by Frostys house. Wen
I herd dogs barking I looked up and saw Clem Baily
go by with his dog team on the road to town and
there was Frosty in the lead. I new Clem wauld not
steal a dog so I new pa had sold dear Frosty to by
us kids Cristmas preasants.

One night I lay awake wondering whether it was fair
to withhold praise from a student who had never known
anything but heartbreak and failure. I decided I would
simply have to risk breaking the spell, come what may,
and tell Auber that his compositions were the best in
the school. In order to accomplish my purpose I kept
him in at recess the following day.

"What did I do wrong, teacher?" he said before I
could speak. A pupil was seldom kept in at recess unless it was for punishment or sickness.

"Why, Auber," I said, "you didn't do anything wrong.
I kept you in simply to tell you that your compositions are the most interesting of all those in the whole
school, including the eighth grade."

Auber's mouth opened in surprise, and his face became suffused with the deepest blush I had ever seen.
I could actually see it start at the neckline and creep
up in a crimson wave until it disappeared into his hair-
line. His soft eyes glistened, then dimmed behind the
tears.

"Oh, teacher," he said in a near-whisper. "Oh, thank
you." No other pupil would have thought to say thank
you. So again I had to make a quick excuse to dash
upstairs before my own tears could show.

February came and with it Auber's sixteenth birthday.
I was relieved when I saw that his parents weren't

going to take him out of school simply because he had reached the legal age beyond which he need not attend. I now dared hope I might guide him through the eighth grade. An eighth-grade diploma isn't much today, but it would probably be an unforgettable milestone in Auber's life—if he made it.

A flu epidemic hit the Wasilla Woods, and at one time I was on the verge of closing the school because absences had nearly reached the halfway mark. Auber and his sisters missed one Friday. Upon their return to school on Monday, Auber was extremely melancholy. *Well,* I told myself, *he'll snap back; this is probably the reaction from the soaring spirits he was in after I praised his work.* Nevertheless, Auber dutifully wrote his composition along with the others that day. I read his somber story after school.

Snow was faling and it was dark in our house even if it still was day time. Angela my baby sister was very sick. Pa had drove to Wasilla in the truk to call the docter in Palmer but the docter said to bring Angela to the hospittle. He wouldnt come to our house.

Angela was in her little birch crib in the corner. Her face was wite and she was to sick to talk. She only laid there and folowed us with her eyes. Ma held her hand and wispered to Pa IT IS SO COLD. Then ma cride and Angelas face was witer then ever and she closed her eyes. Then pa said YOUR LITTLE SISTER IS GONE KIDS. We all cride then. The ground was troze and pa had to get Mr. Fogerty and Clem Baily to help dig the grave. They baried Angela under the big birch by the spring ware she use to play.

Upon inquiry at the store that evening I learned that what Auber had so straightforwardly written had been indeed truth. And it was also true that a doctor from nearby Palmer twenty-six miles away had refused to drive out to the Dubois home. This inhuman monster, according to Marcel Dubois' account, had said over the telephone, "Bring the kid into the hospital, buster; I can't drive way out yunder for a li'l ol' case of sniffles." Yet Marcel had patiently described his little daughter's condition. Marcel Dubois was also said to have sworn that someday he would drive to Palmer and choke the doctor to death right in the middle of the village square.

The sun had burned through the snow on the south slopes of the foothills, and the brown spots were growing into islands amid the diminishing white. The magpies had disappeared—a sure sign of spring; and the huge black-brown moose were edging back toward their summer feeding range in the willow-covered benches beyond the foothills and below the mountains.

Auber was aware of none of these harbingers of spring. While the other children, including his sisters, tumbled out to play at recess and noon, Auber refused to leave his desk.

"Auber," I said softly as he sat there in the room now so bright with the sun streaming in the windows, "maybe if you could talk about Angela to me you would feel better afterward. We cannot bring your little sister back. She wouldn't want you to feel so sad, I'm sure."

Auber's sudden response was actually more than I had expected. It just poured out of him, everything about Angela, from the time she was born until she had died. He ended up quoting his mother upon hearing his father's threats to kill the doctor. " 'You musn't, Marcel, you mustn't; he will pay for his sins like all of us on Judgment Day.' "

After breaking down and telling me all there was to tell, Auber began loosening up again. He wrote one composition which touched on Angela only briefly and indirectly. After that he mentioned his little sister just once.

Everybody spoke low for a long time after my little sister died. My other sisters couldn't got to school that day becaus they couldnt stop crying. Ma cooked and swep and sowed without a word. Pa sawed wood all day but he faced away from Angelas

grave. Junior took me a side and said IF YOU TELL
ANYBODY YOU SEEN ME CRYING I WILL
BLACK YOUR EYES SAVVY. Of coarse I swore
I wouldnt but I said WHAT WILL YOU DO IF
YOU HAPPIN TO THINK ABOUT OUR DEAD
SISTER WEN YOU ARE IN WASILLA
SCHOOL? Junior tride to hold back the tears but
couldnt so he gave me a wolp on the cheekbone and
my eye swoll up and turn black and pa gave him a
licken right after.

Some of Auber's pieces were old happenings, some
very recent. After reading one of them I began to wonder if maybe he wasn't making up some of the
anecdotes he described. For this time Auber had written:

One day pa let Junior go with him into a pool
hall at Palmer. The men playing pool soon found
themselves a ball short. NO WONDER the ball was
in Juniors mouth. Junior could mouth a bigger rock
or egg then me but this here pool ball stumped him.
Revern Ervin was drug in and he said IS YOUR
HOUSE IN ORDER MY SON. Pa said the pool ball
didnt hear a word. Wen Mr. Fabyan poured caster
oil in an empty sardeen can and put it close Junior
made a awfle face and the ball shot out of his mouth
and he threw up. He was mitey tame after that.

Marcel Dubois and his wife, Catharine, called on me in
my home above the school one spring evening when the
sun's low rays were red behind the birches by the lake.
Mrs. Dubois, in common with so many women who had
married men of lower station, had gradually come to
assume a martyr's air. While I made coffee in the
percolator, she said that they had come to discuss
Auber. "We want to thank you, Elizabeth, for being so
patient with Auber. He just adores you, you know.
Sometimes it makes me feel jealous, but I know I
shouldn't. Let's just say I'm a mother and Auber is my
boy."

"That's all right, Catharine," I replied. "Auber needs all of the help he can get from all of us. Lately he is showing signs of becoming an author, and I want to encourage him all I can." Of course, I didn't actually mean there was any chance of Auber's becoming another Mark Twain or a John Steinbeck.

"Author?" exclaimed Catharine Dubois. "Oh, wouldn't that be something! Auber a famous writer."

"Now, mamma," said Marcel. "Please. A farmer, yes, or a carpenter maybe, but Auber can never be a writer. Lizbet just say that to make us feel good."

But I doubt that his wife heard what he said. During most of the visit, she sat there in my old rocker with a faraway, dreamlike expression.

The term was nearing its end. I had become tired of the long Alaskan winters, and since it was obvious that I would never find a husband, I had decided to leave Alaska. I would get a teaching job in California or Florida. But before leaving I would promote Auber to the eighth grade.

Auber began acting uneasy, fidgety; he wouldn't look me in the eye. This was certainly a puzzler. Upon reading his next composition I suspected what was ailing him and I felt sick to my stomach.

Our ranch lies out in the beautiful woods ajacent to the flowery right side of the pitcheresk highway leading west from Wasilla, passing through Bulldozer, and trailing to an end in gorjes Goose Creek Canyon. Our home is a sturdy log stucture with quaint dormer windows which overlook the snowy caps of the incomprabel Chucach Mountains. Queenly birches and stately spruce trees form a heavenly hailo around the flower strewn clearing surrounding our modist home. Our life is a marvlously kalidoscoopic bowl of fun and we live every inch of it to the uttermost hilt. We children play in the sparkling waters of our haply gurgling creek among the brilant-hued rainbow trouts and the shy ferns fringing the silvan banks. The panaramik clouds of spun gold an. . . .

It was ghastly. Auber watched me read and he hung his head in shame. I got him alone as soon as I could and I said, "Auber, don't feel bad. I know your mother told you to say all these things."

His voice came low and I had to strain to hear it. "I tried hard and I memorized it all. I didn't get the words all right, did I, teacher?"

"No," I replied. "You spelled a few wrong, Auber. But I am glad. I don't want you ever ever to let anybody tell you what to write in composition class." I gave Auber a note to give his mother.

*Catharine:* You're not helping Auber this way. You are destroying what it has taken us all year to develop—Auber's sense of achievement, his hard-earned feeling of creative pride. Surely you understand.

But Auber continued to avoid my gaze and he seemed to back deeper into his shell. Finally I gave him a note with instructions for his father.

*Marcel:* Please stop your wife from doing Auber's writing for him. She isn't fooling me and she is harming Auber. Auber is a far better writer than his mother!

I derived a certain smug satisfaction from Auber's next-to-last contribution. It wasn't long, but I thought it was meaty.

The girls was down by the crick ware the trout was sponning. Me and Junior had a porkapine up a tree by the garden stump row. We herd ma and pa geting mader and ma was yeling loud. Sudinly she screemed so loud me and Junior got scaired and run to the house. Pa set on the old rocker holding ma acrost his lap and spanking her. Wen he saw us he said MAMA BET SHE WAS STRONGER THEN ME. Wen he laugfhed ma cride. Wen we got back the porkapine was gone.

The flurry of reports that must always mark the tag end of school term enveloped me so deeply that I was scarcely able to correct all of the papers in time for my final reports. Among the stack of test papers were the last theme assignments for the seventh grade which I had neglected to gather the day before. I plunged into the pile. Auber's contribution ground my frenzied tempo to a halt.

One day we all went to Ankerage with Mr Fogerty in his stachen wagin. Wen we got back home our cow was in the house and the dore was open. Pa swore and yeled WHO LEFT THE COW IN THE HOUSE AND THE DORE OPEN? Nobody oaned up of coarse and pa grabed the rope to leed the cow out but she was to fat becawse she had eat all our potatose in the sack by the backdore. SENSE SHE IS HERE I MIGHT AS WELL MILK HER pa said. Ma got mad and cride agen. The cow slep in the house that night and pa led her out the next day. He said I DON'T SEE WY YOU BALL ALL THE TIME BE-CAWSE I DO THIS SAME THING EVER DAY IN THE BARN. Ma seems to cry mighty easy sense Angela died.

I left Alaska four years ago. Auber has written me many letters since then. He said—— But let him tell it.

*Dear Teacher:* I started eigthe grade and went only one munth. One day Mister Lane said BOY DON'T YOU KNOW ANYTHING? He had asked me wy I dident know any parts of speech and the other kids said AUBER DONT HAVE TO KNOW. Then Mister Lane got mad and yeled. WY DONT AUBER HAVE TO KNOW? HE GOSE TO THIS HERE SCOOL TO DONT HE? Then the other kids got scaired and I dident know what to say. Wen I got home I told pa I wanted to lieve the scool and he said AUBER I DONT LIKE YOUR NEW TEACHER TO. YOU LIEV THE SCOOL AND I WILL TEACH YOU HOW TO BE A GOOD GARDENEER. Mama got mad and went and seen Mister Lane and wen she come home said HOOOMPFF WHAT A FAT DUMMY. I FEEL LIKE TAKEING THE GIRLS OUT OF SCOOL TO. Of coarse she dident.

A year ago Auber wrote again.

*Dear Teacher:* Mr Girsmill is giving me a chanse to work for him at the GOVERMANT EXPEARMINT FARM. He said if I aint lazey as some hes had that I can maybee work steddy. I rote to him for a job and wen he red my leter he drove out to our house and said to pa BY GOD NOW MARCEL I NEVVER KNEW AUBER COULD WRITE. HE IS JUST THE MAN I NEED TO HELP ME RUN THAT DANGED FARM. Then he winked at pa but I saw him. I knew he was teesing me but I was so glad to get my first job that I dident care. And just think I make TWO DOLARS a hour. Ma and pa say put your money in the bank Auber and I tell them I will do that after the girls got deesant close and are famly dont owe a penny to nobody. If it wasnt for you teacher I couldent have wrote a leter to Mr. Girsmill and got a job. I am to bashfle to ask face to face,

Auber's letters have become fewer. But even so I still can't read one but what I see those great brown eyes and that stack of hair—and of course I end up crying.

# DENTON'S DAUGHTER

## BY ELLEN LOWENBERG

📖 📖 📖

With the lousy marks I was getting last January, I really needed something like Denton's daughter, take it from me.

Not that I usually go in for toadying to people or anything, because I don't. Let's put it this way: Mr. Denton was a new teacher, and new teachers are impressionable. I wanted his impression of me to be a good one.

It was actually a very big coincidence that Mr. Denton was my history teacher, because that's where I needed it the most. Luck, I mean. I was just about flunking history. As a matter of fact, I was just about flunking almost everything but math, which was what all the other guys were flunking. It isn't that I'm stupid, it's mainly that I don't work overly hard. And I was going through a special slump then, because of Kathy.

Which leads me from the subject of school to that of Kathy, which is a prettier one but more of a pain in the neck. Kathy and I have been going steady since the ninth grade. She's cute—blond hair, blue eyes, cute nose, cool figure—you know the type. She's smart, too.

Anyway, just about when school started after Christmas vacation, which is when the Dentons moved to town, Kathy and I started having a bunch of little fights. This happens about twice a year, but it always kind of gets me down for a while. It does the same thing to Kathy, I know, because I heard her mother telling my mother that every time we break up Kathy sits around and plays our favorite song on the record player and actually *cries*. Not that I'd ever expect Kathy to admit it to me. Heck, if I sat around and cried over her, you couldn't drag it out of me. Anyway, my marks were hitting an all-time low, and I didn't know what to do about it. Report cards come out at the end of January, so I had one month to patch things up with Kath and get my marks up. At Clinton Carter High, where I go, we get numerical marks, and if my father saw anything below a seventy, I could see myself grounded for the rest of the year. No car. No lacrosse. No Kathy.

So that was the position I was in when the matter of Denton's daughter came up. It all started on Tuesday, when I failed a surprise history quiz. It was practically all dates and names of generals and junk like that. I answered only four questions right, out of ten, and a forty didn't do wonders for my average. As a matter of fact, it brought my average down to sixty-eight. So I thought if I went and told Mr. Denton that I had a strict father, maybe he'd let me do a special report or something to make it up. Not that I usually *ask* for extra work, but if my father were ever to sign a report with a sixty-eight in history (in addition to Heaven knows what in Latin)—the scene is too awful even to consider.

History was last period, so I just kind of walked up to Denton's desk and stood there like an idiot. You could tell he was a new teacher because when he finally looked up he said, "Is there something I can do for you, Carroll?" Nobody ever calls me Carroll. My father used to when he got mad at me, but now he just swears. Truthfully, I'd rather be called any of the various things he calls me than Carroll. It's my father's name, too, and even *he* thinks it's pretty bad. When you get right down to it, I should never have gotten the name at all; it should have been my eighteen-year-old brother's headache, but he was smart enough to get born the week that my grandfather died, so all he got stuck with was Joseph Patrick after my grandfather. They saved Carroll Clement Junior for me. Just my rotten luck. My brother doesn't even use Joseph Patrick—he goes by J. P. because he thinks it sounds cool—J. P. Fahey. Everybody calls me Buck. I don't know how that got started, but my parents probably thought it up because they were sorry for sticking me with Carroll Clement. At school,

most of the teachers call us by our last names, so I'm
used to being called Fahey. I don't mind that, and I don't
mind Buck, but I can't stand the combination Carroll
Fahey, because most of the people I know pronounce it
Fay, and then I'm really in for it. Let's face it, Carroll
Fay does sound fruity. We pronounce it Fayhee, two
syllables. But back to the original point: you could tell
Denton was new at Carter because he called me Carroll.

"It's about that test we had, sir," I said. I didn't want
to get into a long discussion of anything because Kathy
goes to Central High, which happens to be right across
the street from Carter, and I was supposed to meet her
to go to the drugstore for sodas. But I couldn't tell Denton that or else he'd think I wasn't serious about my
schoolwork.

"Sit down, Carroll," he told me, so I did, and then he
looked up and smiled at me and really made me feel
cruddy. He was acting so *nice*. That's another way you
could tell he was new. He opened up his little black
mark book, but I knew he wasn't looking at my marks
because he was looking up at the top of the page; there
are at least ten guys in my class before the F's.

"Fahey," I tried to be helpful.

"Oh, yes, Fahey," he mumbled, and then he *did* find
my marks, because he made kind of a sick face.

"Carroll, your grades have been rather low this quarter. Now, I see that you made an eighty-four last quarter.
Is something the matter?"

That clinched it! About his not knowing how Carter
teachers usually behave, I mean. Can you feature that;
asking me if anything was the matter? Sheesh! That's one
thing you don't get much of from teachers, consideration.
It was almost enough to make me tell him about Kathy,
but I reconsidered; once a teacher, always a teacher.

"Nothing's exactly the matter, sir, only my father will
be very upset if I get a sixty-eight in history and—"

"I don't give make-up tests, Carroll." He was more
on the ball than I thought. "I know you have the ability
to do well, Carroll. Frankly, you puzzle me. I could al-

most believe you don't want to get good grades." I just
looked down at my feet. This wasn't going the way I'd
planned at all. And Kathy'd be mad because I hadn't
showed up yet, and we were on touchy enough ground
to begin with.

"As I said," Mr. Denton went on, "I never give make-
up tests. However, we will have a quiz on Thursday on
chapters twenty-one and twenty-two in the textbook, and
one on Monday on chapter twenty-three. I will average
them with the quiz we had today to make a unit test-
mark, so if you make a perfect score on both quizzes,
the final mark will be an eighty. I think you'll agree that's
fair." I couldn't argue, because it was, so I just thanked
him and got up to leave.

"If it's girl-trouble that's bothering you, Carroll, don't
worry too much. My daughter Evelyn is going through
the same sort of thing." Oh, nuts, I thought. Now he was
going to start talking about his family, and you can't
walk out while a teacher's talking about anything, especially his family. Kathy would really be burning up. That
is, if she was still waiting. She had probably gone home,
or, even worse, but more probably, to the drugstore with
some other guy.

"You see, we just moved to town, and Evelyn hasn't
met many people yet. I'd really like to see her meet
some nice boys and girls—"

That was when it hit me. Hard! It was the biggest
brainstorm I'd ever had, and that's saying something. It
was low-down and sneaky and against all my principles.

"Mr. Denton, if Evelyn could get to a party or two,
she'd probably meet a whole bunch of nice kids. Hey!
Why don't I take her to Artie Hoffman's party Saturday night? She'd like the crowd a lot, they're great kids."
Oh, was that ever a lousy thing to do! Aside from but-
tering up Mr. Denton, I knew that everyone expected
me to take Kathy Anderson to that party, including
Kath. Not that I'd actually asked her, she just figured
I would take her. Who else would I take?

Evelyn Denton, that's who. Mr. Denton would appreciate it; maybe he'd even appreciate it two points worth on my average. Besides, I'd be nice to his daughter. How could a plan like that be bad?

I found out how, about fifteen minutes later, when I met Kathy outside. Denton had thought it over and decided that it would be a good idea. He knew me. He could trust me more than some strange guy he'd never even seen. He gave me his number and I promised to call that night. For a minute there, I actually felt guilty. The guy acted as if I was doing him a favor. He didn't even see through my plan. Not that I wanted him to, but it *was* taking candy from a baby, and I actually liked the guy. Oh, well, I figured, you know what they say about love and war, and with my marks, my father, and Kathy, this was both.

Kathy was waiting in our usual place, and I could tell by that you're-gonna-get-it look on her face that it wasn't going to be exactly fun. What was worse, she plunged right in without giving me a chance to think of anything to say. Not that I usually *can* think of anything to say to Kathy when she's mad. But I'd have liked the chance.

"Okay, Buck Fahey," she snarled, pronouncing it Fay just to annoy me, "you're only half an hour late. I'd like you to know that Kenny Allen asked me to go to the drugstore with him, and so did Marty Tanner, but I turned them both down. And would you like to know why?" If she had dripped sarcasm any more, she would've had to wipe her chin. But she kept right on going, full steam ahead. That's one thing you've got to say for Kathy, once she gets wound up, she doesn't stop. Persistent, that's the word I was thinking of. Kathy's persistent.

"I wanted to stay here to meet *you*, you rat, so I could tell you what I think of you and your phony excuses for always being late. I don't even want to hear this one, because I'm going straight home, and don't bother calling me tonight because we aren't speaking until at least tomorrow. Oh, and by the way, in case we aren't speaking after tomorrow, you can pick me up at eight-thirty Saturday night."

"What for?" I asked like a real idiot. I knew what for as well as I knew my name (which, when you get right down to it, is enough to remember), but that's the way I am sometimes. Especially with Kath. Stupid. Of course, it made her twice as angry.

"For Artie Hoffman's party, you stupid lacrosse player. Don't you have any brain hidden in that brawn?"

"Oh. Artie's, huh? Well, uh—Kathy, I'm not taking you to Artie's because I promised to take my history teacher's daughter."

"You—what?"

"Promised to take Denton's daughter. Aw, come on, Kath, have a heart. The poor kid doesn't know anyone in town. It's probably her first date, and it'll be a big kick for her, going out with a lacrosse player and all. She's probably a real drip; you know what teachers' daughters are like. Straight brown hair, braces, long nose, horn-rimmed glasses, stick figure. It'll be awful to have to spend an evening with her after being used to you, but the poor little weirdo deserves a break." I didn't mean to lay it on quite so thick, but it worked. It was that picture of poor old board-flat Evelyn Denton, crying because she never had a date, that did it.

"Are you sure that she's like that, and that you're only doing this as a favor to her father, Bucky? Are you positive?"

"Absolutely, Kath, I swear. Look, I've got to keep in good with Denton, I don't have a seventy average. If Dad punishes me, we won't be able to meet after school or anything. You know I don't care about this Denton kid—I just pity her."

"Wellllll—okay. I'll forgive you this time, Buck, but just this time. And if you're not taking me out Saturday night, I'll be free to go to the movies with Marty."

"Okay," I said pretty cheerfully. It isn't that I liked the idea of my girl going out with a show-off like Tanner, it's just that I don't usually get off that easy. With Kathy, that is.

That night, I called Evelyn Denton. Her voice didn't sound too bad. Serious, like what you'd expect from a teacher's daughter, but not too bad. I told her to call me Buck because she'd already picked up the Carroll habit from her father. I called Kathy, too, to make sure we were speaking, but she was washing her hair.

The next afternoon when I went to meet Kathy after school, I was in a pretty good mood; at least I knew that she'd be speaking to me. That was my mistake—getting the idea that Kathy's mood would stay the same for more than five minutes. I could tell that something was wrong from that sneaky way that Kathy was smiling at me. I've only seen that kind of smile a few times before, usually on my father.

"Hi, Bucky," she said. There was something about that voice—

"I called you last night, but you were washing your hair," I said. As you can see, it's more or less a habit, this stalling for time. With Kathy, you have to. It didn't work.

"Do you know what else I did last night, Bucky dear? Linda Larson came over for a while, and I showed her that picture of you in your lacrosse uniform that I *used* to carry around in my wallet. So she let me look through her wallet, and I found a picture of a girl in her class, which she very graciously let me borrow to show you." She handed me a color snap of a girl, and—wow! What a looker! Kind of the sophisticated pixie type. Short red hair, big eyes and a figure that you usually can't find on a high school girl. It was all I could do not to whistle a little out of sheer appreciation. Kathy was still being very sweet.

"Naturally, I asked Linda who she was. Would you like to know who she is, Bucky dear?"

"Yeah, who is she?" I was trying not to sound too eager, but it wasn't working too well. Kathy just stared at me, so I asked her again.

"Who is she?"

"*Evelyn Denton,* that's who!" she screamed. I nearly passed out.

"Evelyn Denton? Evelyn—you're kidding! Evelyn *Denton*?"

"Yes, Evelyn Denton, and I see no signs of the braces or the lanky brown hair. And what's more, she doesn't strike me as looking like the shy type, socially or otherwise."

"But, Kathy—"

"As a matter of fact, I would say offhand that she looks quite aggressive."

"But, Kath—"

"If you had told me the truth I might not be so angry, but you *lied*, which definitely proves that there is a lack of trust between the two of us."

"But, Kath—"

"Are you still going to take her out Saturday night?"

"Yes."

"In that case, I have just one thing to say to you."

"But, *Kathy*—"

"Go to—*Hades*, Carroll Clement Fahey Junior!" She turned and tried to walk away the way a movie star would but tripped over her foot and practically fell over, which kind of spoiled the effect. I still had the snap, so I looked at it again.

My first thought was, "After a date with this doll, Kathy'll never speak to me again." But then I had this other thought: "After a date with this doll, what do I care?"

I thought about Evelyn Denton all afternoon. At eight I called her, then I thought about her the rest of the night. I forgot to study for her father's test, so I got an eighty instead of the hundred I needed, but I figured I was pretty safe. Even Denton wouldn't have the heart to fail a guy who would be practically in the family after Saturday night. Friday night, I called Kathy. I figured that after a couple of days' worth of cooling off she'd be willing to make up, but she was out with Marty Tanner. It burned me up, until I looked at Evelyn's picture. Kathy's a real cute kid and all, but this Evelyn was a queen. A real queen. My best friend David Cade had thought so too, when I'd showed him the picture that day.

"Jeez, Buck, she's really got it," he said. "What's Kathy gonna say about her? If I even *looked* at some-one like that, Cynthia would pulverize me." I informed him that Kathy had already had her say.

"Yeah, I can imagine," Dave said kind of pityingly. "But then again, you and that Denton kid could go places." Just then, Cynthia passed, Dave's school ring hanging on a chain around her neck. She tries to wear it a different way each day—sometimes taped up on her finger, sometimes around her neck on a chain, sometimes around her neck on a velvet ribbon. Once I suggested she wear it in her nose like a bull, and she didn't even give me a disgusted look and tell me I could do better than that. It was downright frightening, but I *saw* that look on her face, and I swear, she looked as if she were *thinking it over!* She's pretty, a good dancer, but stupid!

Anyway, Cynthia came by and said, "Hi, Dave, I want to talk to you later." She walked right by and didn't say anything to me, so I could figure out what had hap-pened. She'd been talking to Kath, who had, of course, told her what a lowdown louse I was, so Cynthia wasn't speaking to me either.

"Boy, Kathy must really be furious," David said.

"Aw, Cynthia's just a nut, that's all," I said, not be-cause it had anything to do with the situation, but mostly because, just for that second, I really felt bad about Kathy. Old Dave wasn't even offended because I called his steady a nut. He's used to it.

That afternoon, I smiled at Mr. Denton as I left his-tory. I hoped he hadn't forgotten about the two points on my average. I had forgotten that he'd never said a thing about two points on my average.

I was nervous Saturday night, but I began feeling bet-ter when I got dressed and into the car. I had a pretty long ride out to where the Dentons lived, so I turned on the radio. They were playing this song, *Sweet Little Kathy*.

Do you ever get the feeling that everyone's against you?

The Dentons' house was pretty. Little and white. Not what you'd expect a red-headed bombshell to live in, but because it was so incongruous, it fit perfectly. Incongruous—that's a million-dollar word. Someday I'll have to see if I can't fit it into something I say in school. My Latin teacher'd love it.

I rang the doorbell, and for a minute I hoped that Denton would open the door, because I was in a very polite mood. A lumpy-looking girl in a black velvet jumper answered, and I couldn't help thinking that Mr. and Mrs. Denton must really have some mixed-up genes to have a daughter like Evelyn and one like this, too. She wasn't fat, just lumpy looking, and the black velvet jumper made her look worse. She was wearing box heels and her lipstick was too red. The one pretty thing about her was her shiny, blue-black hair, and she had even ruined that by wearing it in a pony tail with a plastic hair band. If there's one thing I really hate, it's a girl wearing a plastic hair band.

"Hi, Buck," the girl said.

"Hi, Bunky. Where's your sis?"

"I don't have a sister, just a little brother, and besides, what difference does it make where he is?" She gave me a real peculiar look. "Come on, let's go." I was confused, let me tell you. I was just trying to figure it out as a short, gray-haired woman walked in and smiled at me.

"You must be Carroll Fahey," she said, actually pronouncing it right. "I'm Mrs. Denton. I've heard so much about you from George." Then she turned around and said to the girl, "Evelyn, dear, don't stay out too late. Have a nice time, and you, too, Carroll."

Evelyn! I didn't know which end was up, but I suspected that I was on the wrong one. Suddenly, I noticed the mantelpiece; there, next to a bowl of flowers was a blown-up copy of the picture I'd been worshiping for the past two days.

"Who's that?" I blurted.

Mrs. Denton smiled again. "That's my niece, Evelyn Denton. She and our Evvie were both named after the same grandmother. Do you know her, Carroll?"

"I've seen her around," I answered.

I mean, what else could I say?

I still haven't met the beautiful red-headed Evelyn Denton. It seems she goes steady with some Princeton guy. My Evelyn met a boy at the party who's a nut on biology and they've been dating ever since. Kathy didn't speak to me for three weeks. Mr. Denton gave me a sixty-seven in history (the quizzes brought it down one point). He said he was sorry to do it because he had really gotten to like me and I had introduced Evelyn to Lester and all that, but he didn't think personal feelings should enter into grading. Dad hit the ceiling when I brought home my report card and said I couldn't have the car for a month. Which didn't end up much of a punishment because my brother had the measles and, as a final humiliation, I caught them and had a much worse case than my brother.

I could say something in summation of this whole mess, but I won't. For once in my life, I won't.

# HOODS I HAVE KNOWN

## BY SONDRA SPATT

Whenever I reminisce about old beaux, I begin with poor Larry Dinhofer, who sat behind me in the eighth grade and asked me to the P.S. 333 prom because I asked him to my graduation party. From gratitude for that first invitation, Larry's mother bought me a monstrous bottle of Sweet Primrose toilet water, which I have kept to this day. The primroses or whatever they were have become so fermented through the years that I now use it for rubbing alcohol and think "Dinhofer" whenever I have an ache in my back. But strictly speaking, although memorable, Larry was not my first but only my first respectable beau. Before Larry I had an unrespectable romance, long suppressed, a seventh-grade affair with the dirty, untrustworthy Danny Tooey, who was a hood.

Perhaps I should explain about hoods. Hoods in Brooklyn are boys who go to school only by the grace of the truant officer, "hood" being short for "hoodlum." "Juvenile delinquent" is a much longer word and not half as piquant. Our seventh-grade hoods were comparatively unaggressive. They never did much but loaf at the back of the class and throw spitballs at each other, sometimes at the teacher. They wore dungarees or chartreuse pants with pistol pockets in imitation of the Avenue E Boys, who were model hoods and real court cases. Our hoods, although harmless, grew aggressive-looking sideburns and great masses of curly black or blond hair. All of them shaved. Danny Tooey was the biggest, tallest, hairiest of the lot and the one who had been left back most often. He was fifteen.

When Danny was first left back into our class, we ignored each other. Our social milieux, even in school, were different. I sat in the front of the room, covered my books, raised my hand in answer to all questions and agreed with the teacher on all points. I had already set my eye on the General Excellence Award at graduation. Danny, as I have already pointed out, never did anything in school except pledge allegiance to the flag, proving that hoods were untrustworthy but not unpatriotic.

Danny did not cover books; he destroyed them. Miss Malcolm thought well-bound books in hoody hands a waste, so Danny scattered the leaves of his worn-out volumes like nuts in May, sometimes maliciously, more often from the sort of pure disinterest playboys show when they run their Jaguars off cliffs in the movies. No one had ever called upon Danny to read from these books, you see. It was *l'acte gratuit.*

When I fell into disgrace, Danny was the first hood whose friendship I won. I was in with the leader of the gang, so to speak. I had been the Winged Messenger of the seventh grade and scurried around corridors clutching notes from Miss Malcolm with the expression postmen have when they meet up with the sleet or snow or fog people have been telling them about. I took my messenger position seriously, even though the notes, whenever I paused to open them, revealed nothing more serious than a date for tea or a lift to the beauty parlor. One day Miss Malcolm decided to affix a postscript to a note that she'd dispatched with me and came around a corner unexpectedly, giving both of us a shock.

"Since you have proved yourself a criminal, I'm going to treat you that way," she announced pontifically before the class, and made me clean out my desk and remove my books and self to the back of the room.

As a criminal, I found myself in a peculiar position. It had only been a note asking for more toilet supplies for the teachers' rest room, and hardly worth the drastic punishment, I felt. It was a mundane confidence I'd broken, though Miss Malcolm had mysteriously underlined "toilet supplies" for some reason I could not fathom.

Nevertheless, I was disgraced, not only with the teacher but with all my friends. From that day on Miss Malcolm would not call on me in class even though I was the only one who knew the three most important Atlantic fishing ports and waved my arm wildly like a drowning Atlantic fisherman. She instructed the class to ignore me too. My friends from the front of the room, oh, perfidy, had been waiting all these years, I found, praying that I would fall from grace. They simply would not turn their heads or accept my notes.

Instead of being crushed by my fate I was confident and not at all apologetic. After all, I was the star pupil. And what would Miss Malcolm do without me when we reached the difficult Middle Atlantic States? As for my friends, "those schmoey kids" as I called them, my contempt for them was boundless. I vowed if I ever achieved my pure state again I'd make them suffer.

Miss Malcolm seated Danny and me in a double seat, thinking, dear woman, that close contact with a hood was the worst punishment anyone could inflict on a clean, well brought-up little girl. She expected me to cry and beg to be let back, at least to the class middle. That was because Miss Malcolm herself was afraid of that hairy creature who slouched into the class with disquieting tread and rumbled unintelligible answers deep in his throat. "Urghs" was Danny's favorite comment, and it frightened Miss Malcolm.

When I arrived at the last seat, last row, Danny didn't know quite what to think. I was obviously a pseudo hood and not destined to stay very long. Danny didn't rumble anything at me but regarded me mildly, even amusedly, that first afternoon. "You staying here, little girl?" he asked sarcastically as I piled my books in the desk. His tone implied that I didn't look dangerous enough to merit such a position. I don't think Danny fully realized the moral turpitude of note-reading.

No, I didn't think I was going to stay with Danny long either, at first. But days went by, and Miss Malcolm's gaze never glided past the dividing line—Raymond de Fato, who occasionally threw a spitball but wore a tie. I began to grow more and more uncomfortable. The classroom was long and crowded. Because of scufflings and murmurings around me I couldn't hear anything that was going on past Raymond; Raymond wouldn't tell me, and even if I did hear, no one would call on me. But I could not go to Miss Malcolm begging to be let back. I was proud.

I began to bring *Jane Eyre* to school and spent the whole day reading ferociously. But even that splendid book couldn't make up for the fact that I was missing the Middle Atlantic States. Nor did snubbing Miss Malcolm every day in front of the coatroom bring the desired satisfaction. I couldn't complain at home because my mother thought I should beg for mercy. She said I was "a stubborn fool" and "just like your father." I was an outcast and everybody knew it.

I would have been completely miserable if Danny hadn't decided to take me into his group.

Danny began making the first overtures by looking on with me as I read *Jane Eyre*. Of course I was surprised. Until then it had been mere peaceful coexistence. I didn't even know Danny could read. He'd just sat for days looking at me sardonically from under his tousle of black curls. Occasionally he had cocked an eyebrow at me and his entire broad and grimy brow had moved.

"Dat looks like a good book," he said to me one day, looking interested, and I immediately lent him my four-color pencil to doodle with. From then on we were friends. Even the good girls in my class didn't read Brontë because they couldn't understand words like "choler" and "lineaments." Such praise from a hood made me glow with pleasure.

Our friendship was sealed next day, when we had an examination. Danny gave me his rabbit-foot for keeps. It was for luck, he explained, and you could write the answers on a little piece of paper in the claw.

"Are you sure you don't want it?" I remember asking diffidently. "You probably need it more than I do."

"Oh, I can copy off you—dat's all right," he said.

I really didn't want that rabbit-foot. A crib sheet was a little too far out on the road to dishonesty for a former star pupil, and I knew my New England products backward and forward anyway. Still, I accepted the foot for luck and as a token. I still remember the softness of it, and the little sharpnesses that were the nails.

The next thing Danny did was introduce me to the boys. This was difficult, but he managed to get them to ask me to lend them pencils. They were the shiest hoods imaginable. There were really ten of us in the back, but I only got to know five: Danny, Harry la Marca, Alan Brodnik, Ronny Abry and Jo-Jo Begoyne.

These were the Destry Road Boys. Because of his age, ability and the fact that he had been approached by the Avenue E Boys for possible merger, Danny was definitely the leader. He ruled with an iron hand. Once Harry and Jo-Jo had a fight in the back of the room, and they might have ripped each other to pieces if Danny hadn't broken it up. They moved silently, slowly, crouching a little by the door to the gym. "You never seen a shiv fight before?" Danny asked when he saw my wonder afterward, and he showed me the knives, six inches long.

"Dose guys are gonna get into real trouble one day— dey's only tirteen—dey don't have any sense," he said. During the fight Miss Malcolm had gone on with the class in the front of the room as though nothing was happening. After twenty years of dealing with crime Miss Malcolm had found her method—the silent or you-don't-exist treatment.

The boys got a great deal of pleasure out of telling me about shiv fights and how the Avenue E Boys got away with robbing a candy store. The Destry Road Boys had never gotten away with anything because they had never pulled anything, except turning in false alarms, which any five-year-old can do. They were a small-time bunch and they knew it. Our neighborhood, Newton Park, was just too quiet and genteel to start any trouble, and there wasn't any point going over to Avenue E to find some because Danny wouldn't let them. "You want to get your heads knocked off?" he asked. Danny was the most cautious, perhaps because he was the only gang leader I've ever known. He'd been around and he knew that it was safest to do nothing and if anybody asked you anything to just mumble along.

I found that I too could expound to the boys on topics they hadn't heard before, usually last month's lessons. I think I may have been more interesting than Miss Malcolm, because when I told them about Cortes in Mexico and killing the great chief Montezuma, their eyes gleamed and they clasped imaginary sword handles. Alan Brodnik expressed a desire to make a poniard or a rapier in shop that week. "Swords, dat's all you guys need," Danny said in disgust, but I could see that he was interested too.

"Why didn't dey make a deal wit Montezuma and get a percentage?" he asked me once when I got involved with the more intricate dealings. "A percentage is better. Dopey Spaniards." I could see that Danny had everything all figured out.

I had been sitting in the back of the room for a week and a half when I began to notice a perceptible change in Danny. He began to wear white polo shirts instead of his old, saggy yellow one and smelled faintly of Ivory soap. His face was clean and his hair was somehow higher, pulled together into a compact pompadour. Danny even turned his club jacket inside out so that the plain black showed instead of the worn fuchsia silk with its huge black "Destry Boys" lettering. " 'Stoo flashy," Danny said, and that afternoon, after lunch, all the boys had their jackets turned around too.

Soon, whenever Danny and I read together because of Danny's pageless volumes, his fingers curled around my white-clean covers were white-clean too. The fingers also turned the pages exactly right, which proved that Danny could actually read as fast as I did. I began to think that Danny wasn't really a hood, or was just pretending, or that being a hood wasn't so bad at all if only the teacher would notice you. If we listened very carefully, Danny and I, we could hear Miss Malcolm's voice reading *Evangeline* far off, and once, when we got to the part that goes

Black were her eyes as the berry that grows
    on the thorn by the wayside—
Black, yet how softly they gleamed beneath
    the brown shade of her tresses!
Sweet was her breath as the breath of kine
    that feed in the meadows . . .

Danny bent over and whispered. "She looks like you."

Since I was definitely blond and blue-eyed, and since Danny had never whispered before in his life, I began to think something was wrong. Or, if Danny was becoming poetic, something might be right. But anyway—something. Yes, I thought rather priggishly, Danny has probably never sat next to a good poetry-reading little girl in his life; my presence has probably opened the door to a whole new world of clean-smelling respectability.

It occurred to me that I might tame Danny and turn him into a star pupil, thus killing two birds with one stone and getting me a seat in Respectability too. Why, I could probably persuade Danny to take elocution lessons. Then he could learn to pronounce "th" and other things and Miss Malcolm would understand him. I had a little difficulty myself sometimes. And if I could convince his mother to get him some crisp white shirts and a tie. . . . Maybe my mother would iron them for him if Mrs. Toocy was busy.

Ronny, Harry, Alan and Jo-Jo, although they showed no immediate signs of conversion, might still follow their leader out of hood-hood and I would have a whole gang to my credit. I could learn to iron shirts myself. Soon I would walk down Destry Road to be pointed at and stared at by the citizenry. "There's the girl who saves hoods," ladies would say as they waited on line by the fruit counter at Willy's. "Can you come and talk to my boy after school?" "Dere's dat dame." The Avenue E Boys would scowl and lurk behind the gum machine in front of Harry's. "She's the one who's been takin' our best material. Why, Danny Tooey, he could've been the best hood in Brooklyn, he's studyin' for the ministry."

Yes, I would save Danny. I determined to bring my *Believe-It-Or-Not* Ripley book to school immediately so Danny could begin assimilating the mass of interesting facts so necessary to star pupils. We would sit in the first row, side by side.

Alas. While I had been making plans for reformation, I had overlooked the real reason for Danny's behavior, which was, of course, sex. Danny Tooey wanted me to be more than just a friend. On Friday morning, May 11, Danny asked me to go to the movies with him the next evening, May 12. Not in the afternoon. In the evening. It was a sword-fighting picture, he said, and I would like it. I was shocked. Respectable seventh-grade girls, especially me, didn't wear lipstick or go out with boys; eighth-grade girls could wear lipstick and go out, if they didn't make too much fuss about it. But no decent girl ever went anywhere, morning or evening, with a hood.

Oh, yes, there were a few. But they were scrawny and inky-haired and went to P.S. 293 and only appeared hanging around outside by the homogenized-bagel man at three o'clock. They weren't decent either. Because when the boys didn't show up, they would flirt with the homogenized-bagel man, and when he wasn't there they would go to Harry's and stand in front of the gum machine. And they would make remarks like, "Look who's here," whenever someone passed. The Avenue E Dolls, an auxiliary of the Boys, set the fashion in this case, and any girl hood who didn't have long black hair had to grow it or dye it quick, or run the risk of not being à la mode hood. À la mode hood also meant doe eyes, ultrabright lipstick, gold bangle earrings, cheap, tight skirts and the black and white uniform: black bra and white sweater or white bra and black sweater. And no slip. These girls didn't need to wear bras and I did. Only I didn't, and always felt self-conscious when I passed Harry's Candy Store in my light lawn dresses.

No, I couldn't possibly go out with Danny. I might convert him, but I couldn't go out with him. He probably would want me to kiss him in the movies. I knew what

went on in the Destry Theatre; I went every Saturday
night with my mother and father; I knew. Those hoods.
Surely Danny with all his hoodish savoir-faire knew that a
girl in a pinafore dress, long blond braids and well-fed
expression was highly inappropriate for the leader of a
gang. It was just the lure of the unknown, and was, of
course, impossible.

I told Danny politely that I appreciated the thought
but didn't think my mother would let me go out since I
was only eleven years old. I had skipped several grades, I
explained. Danny was very understanding about it and
said I certainly looked older. At the end of the day I gave
him my *Believe-It-Or-Not* Ripley book for keeps, saying
that my mother had refused permission at lunchtime but
that this was for him, blushing all the while, I suppose.
Danny was very embarrassed. He didn't blush, at first
only mumbled "Urghs," but later came over to me at the
coatroom and said: "Tanks. I don't know how to make
just retribution." He was sweet about the whole thing.

Actually, I hadn't told my mother about Danny's invitation at all. I doubted whether she'd think the connec-
tion savory. But I thought about this, my almost first
date, all the way home from school and all weekend. In
fact, I couldn't stop thinking about it. No sooner would I
settle down with my favorite book than the name Tooey
would intrude itself into my mental stream. I felt the irre-
sistible urge to write Danny Toocy, Danny or just plain D.
T. on all my clean book covers. Finally, in desperation, I
wrote Yeoot Ynnad very small in the top of my stationery
box. Such a thing had never happened to me before.

I decided to look up similar occurrences in my library,
my highest source of wisdom. But mine proved an unprecedented occurrence. Heathcliff had been bad and
Cathy had decided to be his girl friend, but he hadn't reformed and they had both died. That was the best I
could find. But still . . . Jane Eyre wouldn't marry Mr.
Rochester when he was already married to Bertha, so it
didn't seem right for me to go out with Danny while he
was still a hood. But after he reformed . . . it would

probably take till eighth grade and then we could go
out legitimately. Girls in the eighth grade not only went
out, they could kiss too.

My mother noticed my mood of sorrowful melancholy,
interspersed with come-hither glances and a slight pucker-
ing motion of the lips, and wrongly attributed my strange
behavior to worry about the Middle Atlantic States. She
instructed me to sue for Miss Malcolm's favor immediately or she would come up to school herself. Poor Mamma.
How was she to know? After all, I had been a terrible
bookworm, and I was only eleven years old.

When I went to the movies Saturday night with my
parents I tried to reconstruct Danny's features. All that
hair made it difficult; it was all I could reconstruct. Underneath Danny was handsome, I decided, and the features of the man on the screen melted, dimmed and
turned Tooeyesque in the darkness. What if it had not
been my father sitting next to me, wheezing slightly from
the air conditioning? What if it had been. . . . To this
day I can give no accurate description of Danny. The
years have blurred even that blurry face. No matter how
handsome and hairy and suave the fifteen-year-old Danny
may have been, I hardly think he could have looked as I
still picture him today—the precise image of Clark Gable.

Coming out of the Destry after the show, I managed
to walk into an embarrassing situation. There stood Alan
Brodnik, leaning against the fire hydrant, his arms
round a girl. Alan looked at me appealingly and removed
his arms. I made no comment, walked by without turning
my head. My heart was sad though, oh, sad. For what
if it had been Yeoot Ynnad?

When I arrived at school Monday morning I found our
back-seat idyl broken. No longer could we peruse the
same book like lion and lamb. Danny and I breathed hard
and stared in whatever direction was opposite; we both
mumbled. At last I had enough courage to ask Danny if
he had learned anything interesting from the *Believe-It-*

*Or-Not* Ripley book. He only looked at me vaguely and mumbled "Urghs." He had retrogressed.

Danny continued shy all day and did not speak to me. But he gave long, piteous glances and drew girls' heads in ink on the backs of his hands. This was terrible. I decided to follow Danny after school and make him talk to me. It was only to find out something of his home life for future reform, I told myself. When three o'clock and Danny and Harry, Jo-Jo, Alan and Ronny broke upon the homogen-ized-bagel man, I was there too.

The boys looked at me curiously. All the other little girls were retreating away from school as fast as they could go, backs straight and heads held high. Was it true? Was it true? Jo-Jo winked at Harry. Danny said nothing but asked me if I wanted salt on my bagel. No, don't buy me bagels, don't, I felt like crying out. I don't *want* to be your girl friend. I just want to find out about your home life. However, I took one with salt.

Danny seemed relaxed and at ease now. He spoke ani-matedly, even vivaciously, and I could catch nearly every word he was saying. He took my arm and headed me, yes, toward Harry's Candy Store. The boys followed. I would not go to Harry's Candy Store, I told myself firmly, I would not under any conditions go to Harry's Candy Store. . . .

On the way to the candy store, Danny told me about his job as utility man, whatever that was, on a small fishing boat out of Sheepshead Bay. The boat and Danny left every day at three in the morning and didn't return till eight-thirty, just in time to drop Danny off for school. "Dat's why I'm so sleepy in da mornings," Danny explains.

When he was sixteen, next year, he wouldn't have to come to school any more and could be a full-time fisher-man. How exciting, I thought, thinking of *Captains Coura-geous*, but then I remembered. If Danny left school, he'd never reach eighth grade, and what would happen to his "th's" and his white shirts and . . . our date for the movies. Even if he became a fisherman—? what if there were a fish famine or something? Without me Danny would have to go back to being a hood. I would not let

that happen. I would persuade Danny not to leave school.
I would go with him to Harry's Candy Store every day
and stand around with him near the gum machine.

When we reached Harry's, there were no girls from 293
around, thank goodness. Danny did nothing worse than
hitch himself up on the wooden rack that held the newspapers and let his feet dangle on the New York *Post*. He'd
been working since he was ten, he said, and it was all
right. Except when the weather was bad and he didn't get
paid. Or just got paid in fish. His Aunt Bella didn't like
fish, he added a little glumly; she hated fish.

Aunt Bella's strong aversion to fish was all I ever
found out about Danny Tooey's home life. "Look who's
here," Danny said next, and when I looked, there stood
Miss Malcolm.

"I want to talk to you, dear," she said.

Miss Malcolm and I walked home together. We had a
long, intimate conversation on the way, though I couldn't
imagine why. I still hadn't apologized, and I certainly
wasn't going to. I suppose Miss Malcolm had come out of
school at three and seen her ex-star pupil in informal
conversation with a recognized hood. Poor Miss Malcolm. She thought she'd been responsible for starting me
on a life of crime.

"You don't know it, dear, but I've been watching you,"
she said. I clutched my stationery box, but she only took
my arm as we crossed the street as though I was her little
girl.

"I've noticed how unhappy you've been at the back of
the room. You've just been moping around and moping
around, haven't you?"

I made no reply. I wondered what Miss Malcolm
wanted me to do for not telling my mother about Harry's
Candy Store. Yes, blackmail was on my mind. I had the
makings of a first-class hood.

"You've been unhappy because you've wanted to come
up to me and apologize for reading my note, haven't
you?"

We were nearing my home. I thought about walking
Miss Malcolm right past it and right on down to Sheeps-

head Bay. We could go down to the pier and watch the fishing boats come in. My Lord, I really was a fiendish child, now that I think of it.

"But you've been afraid. You've been afraid I was going to say something unkind, weren't you?"

She patted me kindly on the arm. I thought of how I had walked past her every morning on my way to the coatroom, my head held high.

"But you know, I wouldn't have said anything unkind. Because I like you, dear. I think you're my best pupil."

I still didn't say anything. I was her best pupil. I wondered what Miss Malcolm was planning to study next. It must be something harder than the Middle Atlantic, because three people had raised their hands that day and she didn't need me.

"And because I know you've wanted to apologize for a long time, tomorrow morning I am going to let you come back to the first seat, first row."

I couldn't stop the pleasure that I felt.

I didn't know why I had been reinstated but I was glad. Justice, as I had always maintained, does triumph. And oh, what I would do to all those schmoey kids. I was a nasty-good little girl.

Miss Malcolm came inside the house to meet my mother and we all had tea. I didn't mind taking the enemy inside. Danny would approve, I was sure. And from my influential position, what couldn't I do for my friends. Soon I would convince Miss Malcolm of Danny's merits—and then. . . .

"Do you think seventh-grade girls are too young to go out?" I remember asking Miss Malcolm as Mamma poured tea.

Alas, again. All my plans were in vain. The end of the affair came next day.

As Miss Malcolm announced the happy news and I carried my books away from our scarred double seat to my honored one, Danny stared at me sullenly without saying a word. He didn't say good-by, but on my last trip to the front of the room he piled his *Believe-It-Or-Not* Ripley book on top of my grammar and the stationery box with the secret Yeoot Ynnad. He looked at me as though from across a million rows of double seats. Then he turned back to carving his name on the desk.

Hurt and bewildered, I couldn't understand Danny's heartlessness. I followed him out of the school building at three, lingered shyly by the homogenized-bagel man, but he just walked away. His back was slouched and his hair was no longer kempt. He was whistling.

After this I never went near Danny or any of the other boys again. And when Larry Dinhofer asked me for a date to the senior prom I pretended that he was the first. But I always kept track of the Destry Road Boys, secretly, ashamedly. I felt a strong sense of communion with them and liked to think that my short stay had done them all good. Alan and Ronny and Harry went on to high school with me, but were put in special RX classes where they could sit around all day and throw spitballs without being disturbed by anyone. They just had a happy, lazy time. Occasionally I'd glimpse them having refreshments in front of the school. It was a different, nonhomogenized-bagel man, but the same boys all right. When I passed they would stare but never make any sign of recognition.

Although none of the Destry Boys ever made Honor Society or anything like that, they never got any more delinquent than they were. As it turned out, only one boy from P.S. 333 ever ended up in jail, and that was Larry Dinhofer. He robbed a liquor store, and he had always worn white cuffs and sat in the first row, and no one I know has ever found a logical explanation. So Larry does belong among the hoods I've known after all. Alan Brodnik, bless him, was the only Destry Boy whose degenerate career I followed after high school. I've lost touch with him since, but the last I heard he'd turned up at Brooklyn College carrying *Tropic of Capricorn* and wearing a neat black goatee and a red velvet cummerbund. I never could quite understand that one either.

As for Danny, I never saw him after graduation. In fact, I don't think he stayed around that long but left after his sixteenth birthday sometime in March. I believe he gave the Destry Road Boys to Jo-Jo because he was the smartest. By that time my wounded feelings had healed, since I'd decided what had motivated him. It was all due to Danny's pure moral philosophy or something, I deduced, that was stronger than mere romance. Hoods didn't do anything but pledge allegiance to the flag. Star pupils sat in the first row. We just couldn't be friends. It was against all established codes, and Danny supported codes. I had to admire that.

Someone I know says she thinks she saw someone who looked like Danny in a summer theatre production in Woodstock last year. She said that he was still big and had a lot of hair but that he spoke English perfectly. She said he was sweet and looked like Marlon Brando. Despite what my friend says, I don't like to think Danny became an actor. I don't like to think that at all. It makes me sad and a little embarrassed, for that would mean after all my seventh-grade heartbreak and eleven-year-old plans somebody else had reformed Danny after all. I'd rather have him be a fisherman. I'd rather have him be a hood.

# PLANET OF THE CONDEMNED

### BY ROBERT MURPHY

❏ ❏ ❏

Neither of them said anything until they had walked halfway across the field from the launching pad and then, as though at a command, they both stopped at the same time and turned to look back at the rocket. Though each of them was aware of the other's action, they looked first before they spoke of it. They were caught up for the moment in spite of themselves by the great sleek shape there beside the gantry, the soaring lean thing which towered up beyond the glow of the lights until it was lost in the gloom and could only be estimated fully by its pattern of a more complete blackness which blotted out a few stars. That outline, in the light and above it, held their eyes and their thoughts with its somehow fatal cleanness of line; it had the air of being beyond the power of man, although he had made it and would fire it and claimed he could control it with the devices that he had invented and made and put into it.

"Well," the shorter, darker man, Alec Moncrief, said. "You stopped walking too, Bozy." He looked at the other man with his head canted a little to one side, with a faintly mocking and sardonic air. "Could it be that you have reservations about our enterprise?"

"I guess I do," Jerry Bozemann, the other man, said. "As many rockets as I've seen go off, as many of them as I've been in, I still have the feeling inside me somewhere that we don't really decide where they're going, that they decide it for themselves. Usually they string along with us, but once in a while they get tired of that and have notions of their own, and then we call it a malfunction."

"But mostly they humor us, huh?" Moncrief said and grinned. It was a tight grin, private and personal, and

118

like the canted head seemed a little sardonic. "You're certainly philosophical tonight, Bozy," he said and started to walk again.

Left behind, Bozemann took a little skip and caught up. He was a friendly man and had hoped that now they had been inside the rocket there would be a feeling of complete rapport between them; it stung him to be held off and treated as though he had said something rather foolish. "Go ahead and laugh," he said, and gestured toward the low line of lights they were heading for across the field. "You probably won't be doing much more laughing after we get back there and find out why they encouraged us to come out here and look at the rocket by ourselves."

"It was a little unusual, wasn't it?" Moncrief asked. "A delicate attention. You know as well as I do why they did it. They wanted to give us a chance to size up all those new control devices and wonder why they were there and then realize in decent privacy that maybe we won't be coming back."

Bozemann was silent for a long moment as they walked. "Yes," he said finally and gave a half-audible sigh. "It sounds like that's it."

"And now you feel dubious about being a hero?"

"No," Bozemann said. "I volunteered and I want to go."

"I thought I heard a regretful sigh."

"I met a girl not long ago," Bozemann said quietly, "and learned that I'd never really met a girl before."

"So," Moncrief said. He started to say something else, glanced at Bozemann in the gloom and felt rather than saw something about him that made him check himself. He changed the subject. "I was thinking of a different sort of thing," he went on. "More on the line of your rockets that get unconventional notions, like faithful old dogs that have behaved themselves for years suddenly getting ideas of their own and upsetting the applecart. My grandfather was one of those characters back at Cape Canaveral in the 'Fifties, when they first began to work out on rockets, and they decided to send off a few mice.

They didn't know anything in those days; there was a great uproar about getting men on the moon before our friends the Russians did it, and they wanted to see if they could find out about belts of radiation and so on. Whether the mice would get back alive, and what the effects on them would be. That kind of thing. They were in a hurry and pretty ignorant, like curious monkeys that didn't know what they were doing—and God knows whether they caused any trouble somewhere out in space. Later on they sterilized their payloads, as you may recall, to avoid the chance of contaminating anything.

"Anyhow, these jokers decided they wanted two laboratory mice and two wild mice, and my grandfather elected me to catch the wild ones. I was only a kid, of course, and I was flattered at being a partner in the great enterprise. I knocked myself out to catch the nasty little things and finally I got a pair of them. I was pretty proud of them and I thought they ought to be grateful to me for giving them the chance to be the first mice in space, but they weren't. One of them even bit me. I wasn't so proud of them after that. I got mad at them. I gave them electric shocks to get even and finally cut half an inch off their tails."

"Why?" Bozemann said in a startled tone. "That was a cruel thing to do."

"Sure, so it was a cruel thing to do," Moncrief said. He said it rather absentmindedly, for he recalled now, after all these years, that he hadn't caught the mice himself. A neighbor's boy, with whom he used to play, had caught them and he had got them away from the other boy and taken all the credit himself. That had been the first time, he remembered, that he realized what suckers people were; it had been a very useful discovery, and he had used it ever since. He pulled his mind back. "At any rate," he said, "up the mice went in the rocket, but they never came down. There was an elaborate setup to recover them but they didn't re-enter. That rocket had ideas of its own, and nobody knew where it went. Odd you reminded me of that, isn't it?"

Bozemann didn't reply. He turned his head and looked

at Moncrief in a puzzled way, frowning a little, and then looked to the front again. They were almost to the low building now; the lights, shining softly through the windows, revealed their faces to each other, and Moncrief saw Bozemann's expression.

"We seem a little far apart in our meditations," he said, "but it won't make any difference in a few minutes, when we get inside and they give us the word."

"I suppose not," Bozemann said, still thinking about the mice, "but I'd rather have my mental baggage than yours. I'll admit it's softer, but it doesn't seem so lonely."

Moncrief grinned again with his faintly sardonic air and didn't reply. He reached the door first and pulled it open and held it. "After you, friend," he said in a mocking tone. "In you go. I'll trail along behind, upheld and comforted by your invisible cloak of illusions."

Bozemann went through the door, and Moncrief followed him. There was a lanky soldier standing there waiting for them. He saluted. "The C.O. wants you in his office right away, sirs," he said. "Please follow me."

The soldier started out; Moncrief looked at Bozemann and raised his eyebrows, and they fell in behind the soldier. There weren't many people about in the bare, green-tinted corridors at that hour of the night; they all nodded at the two men with a careful casualness and after they had passed turned to look after them. They somehow built up an atmosphere of tension that the two men became aware of; soon they fell into step with the soldier and held it until Moncrief, realizing that they were doing it, deliberately broke the cadence.

They came to General Blunt's door and the soldier knocked, pushed the door open and stood aside. They went in. The general was sitting behind his desk, poker-faced, ruddy and rumpled as usual; another man, a stocky stranger with shining glasses and red hair, dressed in a coverall, sat off to the right.

"Morning," the general said. "Major Moncrief, Major Bozemann . . . Doctor Kost." The three men shook hands. "Doctor Kost will fill you in. Sit down."

The two rocket men took chairs, looking at Kost with

that veiled quizzical and superior look of men of action when they are confronted with the sedentary egghead who invents the devices in which they risk their necks.

"I will be brief," Kost said with a shadow of an accent when they had taken chairs. "There is no need to elaborate upon the details, which are very technical." He sounded a little pedantic and smiled slightly as though to apologize that he was a scientist and they were not. "We think there is a planet in our system that was unknown until recently. This seems impossible to you, but we think it is so. It cannot be seen by optical telescopes and is only suspected by radioastronomy, on which it gives only occasionally what we call a 'ghost,' which we often thought perhaps was a malfunction. But of late we have devised a new spectroscope, a very secret device so far unknown to others, and with this spectroscope we get from this planet a new line which indicates that there is on this planet an element not known to us."

He paused, and Moncrief and Bozemann stared at him. For a long moment there was a silence in the room. Suddenly Kost moved forward in his chair and his glasses glittered; a cool, forensic enthusiasm took hold of him. "Why could it not be so?" he asked. He raised one hand and cupped it before his face. "There is still much we have not found out. It is as if this element acts upon light, repels it or bends it." He dropped his hand. "Perhaps other particles as well. This would seem to confirm why we cannot see it by optical telescopes and it gives only the occasional ghost by radioastronomy. We are not sure; we have only the hypothesis. But this planet, we think it is not too far. There was no guidance system to reach it, but now we have devised one to use the new spectroscope."

He ceased speaking and leaned back in his chair. The silence fell again, but this time it was different. Moncrief and Bozemann knew where they were going now: far out across the terrible gulfs of lonely space toward a thing unknown and mysterious, uncertain, only guessed at, and possibly very lethal. Bozemann, after a startled look at Kost, had dropped his glance and was now contemplating the floor. Moncrief looked at the general, who looked back at him.

"So that's it," Moncrief said.

"That's it," the general said. "We need this stuff, if it's there. And, crowded and edgy as the world is, we need it first. If it repels light, as they think it might, there isn't any other rocket propellant that could touch it. Or——"
He shrugged; there were too many other intangible and unimagined possibilities. "If it's there," he said, "if it is a planet and not a cloud of radioactive particles or dust or devil knows whatnot." He picked up a pencil lying on the desk and tapped it softly on its unsharpened end. "Now," he said, "this is a good rocket, well supplied with everything we think you'll need. So far as we can foresee, if there's a planet and it isn't too far you'll land on it and be able to get back. If there isn't, the conventional guidance system will take over and bring you home. You know as well as I do how chancy it is; the imponderables run very high; this is a puzzle, as some old joker said once, wrapped in a mystery inside an enigma. Do either one of you want to pull out now?"

"No," Moncrief said quickly. "No, sir."

"How will we know what to look for, general?" Bozemann asked. "We wouldn't know this new element."

"Doctor Kost is going with you."

They both turned and looked at Kost with a new and rather reluctant approbation. He flushed slightly and dropped his glance.

"Doctor," Bozemann said, "you found this thing. If you'd give us a clue what to look for you wouldn't have to go."

"Might turn out to be uncomfortable," Moncrief said, suddenly getting his faintly sardonic air back again.

Kost raised his head, looked at Moncrief and smiled. "It might, major," he said. "Possibly I am the only one who knows how uncomfortable. Thank you for your kindness, but I will go."

The general, who had been listening to all this, said, "You will all be ready to go within the hour?"

They all straightened involuntarily in their chairs, and

rather self-consciously relaxed again, nodding as the general's eye moved to each of them in turn. He picked up the phone and said, "Give me Macauley. Macauley? General Blunt. Start your countdown. They'll be at the pad in about an hour." He hung up, gave each of them a long, searching look, and arose like a man with a weight on his back, slowly. They jumped to their feet, and he shook hands with each of them. "Be at the front entrance in forty-five minutes. Suits and all that. You'll have time to write a short note or two if you hurry. Don't worry about your dependents." For an instant he lost his poker face, swallowed, and got it back again. "Good luck," he said and turned away as they filed out.

After he'd got into his suit, Bozemann looked at the girl's picture on the bureau for a long moment and opened the top bureau drawer and took out several sheets of paper and a pen. He looked at the picture again, touched it gently, and put the paper back and closed the drawer.

In the next room Moncrief finished zipping himself into his suit, stretched to settle himself, and looked at the photograph on his own bureau. It was a cracked and faded picture of his grandfather. His parents had liked neither him nor each other, and the sardonic defenses he had built against them and after them against the rest of the human race didn't extend to the old man, whom he had loved. Hampered by the suit, he saluted the picture. "Good-by, old boy," he said. "Maybe I'll find your mice for you." Then he went out the door.

Doctor Kost was waiting for them, and a car took them across the field. The first wan streaks of dawn were in the sky, and in the dim and chilly light technicians were swarming about the gleaming rocket. The crew chief went up in the elevator with the three of them and into the capsule crammed with gear, checking their fastenings for them, seeing that their food tubes were within reach, his eyes moving rapidly about over the improbable multiplicity of dual banks of dials and gauges, TV screens and control knobs within reach of Moncrief and Bozemann. Then he backed toward the door. "Happy landings, you all," he said diffidently in a soft Alabama drawl. "If the light turns red, put your masks on. The jets are about warm enough, and I reckon you'll take off in about twelve minutes. 'Bye, now." The airlock door closed behind him, and they heard the locks click.

They lay silently and withdrawn into themselves on the cushioning plastic foam, not speaking, setting their teeth and their muscles and bones, and then the noise began with a click that immediately swept into a roar that filled the world and howled up beyond belief. In the shattering cataclysm of sound the foam fought to crush them flat, and then blackness took them for a time.

At first, after the final blast and jar of landing, they lay still and listened to the faint crackling of the cooling jets in the silence, like swimmers who have crossed a wild welter and chop of tide rips and currents to a shore they did not really think could be achieved. Moncrief was the first to move. He folded back the control for the rocket's landing legs, unstrapped himself, sat up and looked at Bozemann. "Well, Bozy," he said. "Well, Argonaut. It looks as though you'll make it back after all."

"Congratulations, major," Bozemann said, letting out his breath in a long exhalation. "You're a sterling pilot. You'll be promoted for this. Are you all right, doctor?"

"Yes," Kost said, sitting up. "Yes, I am fine. It is astonishing, is it not? How long does the ringing in the head last?"

"A day or so," Moncrief said. "There are God knows how many million decibels to shake out. Maybe we'd better look outside and see what we've bought."

Like children coming downstairs on Christmas morning they moved to the airlock. The inside door had a panel of heavy unbreakable glass, and they gathered before it. Moncrief touched a switch and the outside door swung open. The widening aperture was flooded with pinkish light; and as the door swung wide and locked, a section of their new world was before them: a long calm meadow ending in a wood, sloping uphill, of gi-

gantic trees bigger than the oldest redwoods of earth.
The trees were pinkish too, like the meadow, but a little
darker than the light, and they couldn't see the hill's top;
a mist lay over it, or what seemed to be a mist—a
crepuscular diffusion that appeared to absorb light
rather than blot it out. All within their view was strange
to them because of the color of the light, but calm and
untroubled and beautiful, like a happily remembered
afternoon on earth bathed by the rosy glow of early sun-
set. It caught at their throats like the nostalgic memory
of a perfect thing that was a little melancholy because
the mind had known it couldn't last or be repeated.

They all stared spellbound at it until Moncrief moved
and looked at the instrument panel beside the door. "No
harmful radiation," he said. "And there's air out there. A
little high in carbon dioxide, but not too high. We'll have
to take it easy when we go out. Temperature, seventy degrees. It looks like a place to retire to, Bozy." He turned
to Bozemann and saw tears in his eyes, and turned away
again. He felt close to tears himself, and fought the feeling
down. The place was so still, so dreamlike in its cleanli-
ness and calm after the uproar and bustle and confu-
sion of the overcrowded earth that it brought to him
with terrible force the realization that Bozemann had
memories and a goal and he had neither, that he had
missed or misused too many things in his life.

He let this realization wash over him for a moment and
then set it aside with a muttered curse. There was no use,
he thought, of crying over spilled milk; the thing to do,
now that they had landed upon this planet which no one
had ever thought they would even find, much less make a
landing on, was to get the credit. Not part of the credit,
but all of it: the credit, the promotion and the acclaim.
He gave his two companions a quick glance from under his
eyebrows and thought of all the others who had been
outmaneuvered; simple fellows who had gone down as
he had come up. Kost meant nothing to him; he had
liked Bozemann, but that was beside the point now. "If
you've looked at the scenery long enough," he said,
"we'll have a council of war and get to work."

Bozemann and Kost looked at him without speaking and they went back and sat down on their couches. "Doctor," he said to Kost, "we've got you here. What do you want to do first?"

Kost looked at him for a long moment, with a little frown. "There are more things than I can count," he said, "and many of them are not practical. I did not think I would ever feel this way. However, when I see the fog, the strange mist on the hill that swallows the light, I think perhaps the element is there. Perhaps there are rocks up there, with the element. I will go up there. If we are in a hurry——"

"We are in a hurry," Moncrief said, "according to the general. The next time you come you can stay as long as you please. I'd better report." He got up and moved to the corner where the ultrashort-wave radio was installed, switched on the power, and put on the headset. "Base Seven," he said. "Base Seven. Argonaut here, Argonaut here. All's well." He shut off the power and took off the headset and came back to his couch. "They wanted it kept short," he said, "in case our energetic friends happened to suspect or had this channel. They'll monitor us until we get back, but I doubt we'll send again. Now, doctor, we'll fit you out."

They all stood up and moved to the cabinet on the wall and took out Kost's gear: a Geiger counter, a machine pistol, a hammer and metallic bag for samples and a belt radio with its light headset. They helped him stow it all, loaded the pistol's magazine and showed him how it worked.

"Hadn't I better go with him?" Bozemann asked.

"I was coming to that. Go to the edge of the woods, but don't go in. Stay in the open where I can see you and you can see all around you. If Doctor Kost shoots or yells 'Mayday!' don't go in. Signal me or fire a burst and come back here fast. Not," he said, turning to Kost, "that I want to desert you, doctor, but I think it better we get together if you have trouble. You should come out or make contact with Bozy in two hours at the outside. Is everything clear?"

Kost nodded; Bozemann picked up another machine pistol and loaded it, and they went to the airlock and down the ladder to the ground, which was scorched in a great circle by the blast that eased them down. Beyond this charred circle the ground was covered with a sort of pinkish-gray giant moss as high as a man's knees. Here and there great leafy plants grew out of it, bearing strawberry-like fruits as big as automobiles. They had landed on a height of land within a sort of huge cup; at its edges, falling away to a great distance except where the woods they had first seen thrust out toward them, the country rose up covered with the great trees and was finally lost, cut off by the mist. There was a high, faintly tinted thin overcast which hid the sky, and the air, scented with a strawberry fragrance, was so winy and light that it almost seemed to sparkle in the nose.

Looking over the lovely wide view, filling his lungs with the wonderful air, Bozemann stood bemused by the dreaming calm beauty of this world and wished that he could bring his girl here and stay forever. He was well aware that idyls don't last, but he would be very willing to chance starting over here rather than fill out his life on the crammed and hurried and frightened earth.

Moncrief had been carefully looking over the whole wide circle of their view with binoculars and had seen nothing; not an animal, not an indication of habitation. He turned to Bozemann. "Dreaming again, Bozy?" he asked. "There's nothing here but vegetation that I can see, and it's time to go. Try the walkie-talkie from a hundred yards out or so."

"We can look as we walk," Kost murmured on the other side of him. "I, too, would like to stay in this place."

They started out through the moss, which was springy but firm enough to make walking not too difficult and which had a faint, unusual fragrance of its own. Moncrief watched them go. At a hundred yards or so they stopped and signaled that they were trying the radio, but he couldn't hear anything; when he tried to talk to them

Bozemann threw his hands into the air to indicate that
it was useless, and they went on. He watched them
stop at one of the plants and try the fruit; they ate more,
and he knew by their gestures to him that it was delicious.

It took them quite a while to cover the five or six hundred yards to the trees; and after they had reached them
and Kost had gone in, he watched Bozemann move calm-
ly up and down at the wood's edge for a while and went
into the rocket to get his camera and another pistol.

When he came out again Bozemann wasn't there; he
had gone. A feeling of irritation took hold of Moncrief.
He had planned to wait a few minutes, walk casually across
the meadow to Bozemann, cut him down with a surprise
burst from the machine pistol and dispose of his body
under the moss. Neither Bozemann nor Kost could be
left alive on the planet; it would be too awkward if they
survived until the next rocket landed. Kost, when he
came out of the trees again, would be no problem; the
problem was where Bozemann had gone.

Moncrief's irritation, fed by his nervous distaste over
what he intended to do, began to mount. He coldly con-
trolled it by telling himself that Bozemann would soon
reappear, but time began to draw out and there was no
sign of him. An hour went by, and at the end of it Moncrief had grown puzzled and apprehensive. He couldn't
decide what to do. Their agreement had been so simple
that neither of them could have misunderstood it; Bozemann had stood in the open, and if any sort of trouble
had appeared he would have come back or fired a burst
with the pistol. He had his dreamy moments, but even
when he was having them his awareness was always on a
hair trigger and his reflexes were extraordinarily fast;
Moncrief had been in enough tight spots with him to be
completely confident about that. If there was something
intangible and malign in this place, an influence unknown
to man, a thought that had power to reach out and
pluck a man out of sight——

Moncrief shuddered and cursed and steadied himself;
he realized that the lovely world about him had not

changed except in his mind, and he brought his mind
back to sanity. If anything had got hold of them it
would have got hold of him too; anything, he thought
suddenly, except the fruit they had eaten and he had
not. Perhaps it had contained a poison slow enough so
that it had not felled Bozemann until he had returned
to the rocket, and Bozemann was lying doubled up on
the moss now where he couldn't see him. There was no
other answer, or Bozemann would have signaled. He
raised the binoculars and studied the woods. He couldn't
see very far into them; they were shadowed and leafy
and there was undergrowth; but nothing moved in it.

Then he recalled that he had set a two-hour limit.
Perhaps, he thought, he should wait that long. It could
be that Kost had found something he wanted help with
not very far in and had called Bozemann to give him a
hand. But wouldn't Bozemann have waited for him to
come out of the rocket and indicated what he was going
to do? It wasn't like Bozemann to act against the agreement.

Moncrief was a steady man—in any mundane circum-
stance too sardonic and cynical to be upset—but the
circumstances weren't mundane. He was alone and very
far from home, in a world completely unknown and un-
fathomed, and he didn't know what to do. He couldn't
blast off at once and return to report that he had been
on a lovely, empty world with mist on the hills into
which two men had vanished and that he hadn't investi-
gated; he couldn't go off and leave them. How long
should he wait? Should he leave the rocket and cross
the meadow to see if Bozemann was lying on the moss?
It would be a much better solution if he was; but what
if he wasn't?

He had so far kept a tight hold on his mind, but in his
dilemma the terror that lies in the unknown crept in
upon him. He held off with great difficulty the feeling
that there was—*something*—in the great towering woods,
watching him. The hair on his neck stirred, and he
realized that his breathing had become more rapid. It

had the effect of filling him with a sudden, consuming rage.

He started across the field toward the spot where he had last seen Bozemann. After a few steps he began to trot. He had gone about fifty yards when a gray shape emerged from the woods, and then another. From the right and the left others came out, suddenly appearing. Some were white, like laboratory mice, and some were piebald. They *were* mice, and for a moment his startled mind, confused by the great size of the trees, didn't realize that they were as big as dinosaurs.

As he turned to run, however, his mind became cool and practical again and corrected their scale—and he realized their size. He saw by a snatched glance over his shoulder as he ran that they were all making for him at great speed and that it would require half an hour at least to prepare the jets to warm and fire and that surely would not be enough; for the ruinous gift that he and his grandfather in their ignorance had given this planet had so increased in size through mutations and the growth rules of the place that it—they—wouldn't be long held off by the rocket's thin shell.

He panted up the ladder and touched the switch to close the airlock door and ran over to the switch that started the jets warming and touched that. He had just got himself braced into the corner where the radio was and switched it on and started to speak into it when the first creature struck. The rocket quivered and great claws scratched upon it, and then there were increasing shocks and clawings as they swarmed over it and overbalanced it and knocked it down, and then their teeth went to work on it.

The two men monitoring the rocket's channel leaped to their feet and stood aghast as Moncrief's voice came in over the speaker, across empty space, desperately fast against a shattering metallic clamor that filled the radio room. ". . . world of a dream, do not try to reach it . . . grandfather . . . they were in too much of a hurry, they didn't. . . ." His voice ended in a thunderous crash and

a roar of shrill and blood-curdling squealing, and then
even the carrier wave went dead.

The two men stood staring at each other, white-faced
in the sudden silence.

# TEST

### BY THEODORE L. THOMAS

꧁   ꧁   ꧁

Robert Proctor was a good driver for so young a man. The Turnpike curved gently ahead of him, lightly travelled on this cool morning in May. He felt relaxed and alert. Two hours of driving had not yet produced the twinges of fatigue that appeared first in the muscles in the base of the neck. The sun was bright, but not glaring, and the air smelled fresh and clean. He breathed it deeply, and blew it out noisily. It was a good day for driving.

He glanced quickly at the slim, grey-haired woman sitting in the front seat with him. Her mouth was curved in a quiet smile. She watched the trees and the fields slip by on her side of the pike. Robert Proctor immediately looked back at the road. He said, "Enjoying it, Mom?"

"Yes, Robert." Her voice was as cool as the morning. "It is very pleasant to sit here. I was thinking of the driving I did for you when you were little. I wonder if you enjoyed it as much as I enjoy this."

He smiled, embarrassed. "Sure I did."

She reached over and patted him gently on the arm, and then turned back to the scenery.

He listened to the smooth purr of the engine. Up ahead he saw a great truck, spouting a geyser of smoke as it sped along the Turnpike. Behind it, not passing it, was a long blue convertible, content to drive in the wake of the truck. Robert Proctor noted the arrangement and filed it in the back of his mind. He was slowly overtaking them, but he would not reach them for another minute or two.

He listened to the purr of the engine, and he was
133

pleased with the sound. He had tuned that engine himself over the objections of the mechanic. The engine idled rough now, but it ran smoothly at high speed. You needed a special feel to do good work on engines, and Robert Proctor knew he had it. No one in the world had a feel like his for the tune of an engine.

It was a good morning for driving, and his mind was filled with good thoughts. He pulled nearly abreast of the blue convertible and began to pass it. His speed was a few miles per hour above the Turnpike limit, but his car was under perfect control. The blue convertible suddenly swung out from behind the truck. It swung out without warning and struck his car near the right front fender, knocking his car to the shoulder on the left side of the Turnpike lane.

Robert Proctor was a good driver, too wise to slam on the brakes. He fought the steering wheel to hold the car on a straight path. The left wheels sank into the soft left shoulder, and the car tugged to pull to the left and cross the island and enter the lanes carrying the cars heading in the opposite direction. He held it, then the wheel struck a rock buried in the soft dirt, and the left front tire blew out. The car slewed, and it was then that his mother began to scream.

The car turned sideways and skidded part of the way out into the other lanes. Robert Proctor fought against the steering wheel to straighten the car, but the drag of the blown tire was too much. The scream rang steadily in his ears, and even as he strained at the wheel one part of his mind wondered coolly how a scream could so long be sustained without a breath. An oncoming car struck his radiator from the side and spun him viciously, full into the left-hand lanes.

He was flung into his mother's lap, and she was thrown against the right door. It held. With his left hand he reached for the steering wheel and pulled himself erect against the force of the spin. He turned the wheel to the left, and tried to stop the spin and career out of the lanes of oncoming traffic. His mother was unable to right herself; she lay against the door, her cry rising and falling with the eccentric spin of the car.

The car lost some of its momentum. During one of the spins he twisted the wheel straight, and the car wobblingly stopped spinning and headed down the lane. Before Robert Proctor could turn it off the pike to safety a car loomed ahead of him, bearing down on him. There was a man at the wheel of that other car, sitting rigid, unable to move, eyes wide and staring and filled with fright. Alongside the man was a girl, her head against the back of the seat, soft curls framing a lovely face, her eyes closed in easy sleep. It was not the fear in the man that reached into Robert Proctor; it was the trusting helplessness in the face of the sleeping girl. The two cars sped closer to each other, and Robert Proctor could not change the direction of his car. The driver of the other car remained frozen at the wheel. At the last moment Robert Proctor sat motionless staring into the face of the onrushing, sleeping girl, his mother's cry still sounding in his ears. He heard no crash when the two cars collided head on at a high rate of speed. He felt something push into his stomach, and the world began to go grey. Just before he lost consciousness he heard the scream stop, and he knew then that he had been hearing a single, short-lived scream that had only seemed to drag on and on. There came a painless wrench, and then darkness.

Robert Proctor seemed to be at the bottom of a deep black well. There was a spot of faint light in the far distance, and he could hear the rumble of a distant voice. He tried to pull himself toward the light and the sound, but the effort was too great. He lay still and gathered himself and tried again. The light grew brighter and the voice louder. He tried harder, again, and he drew closer. Then he opened his eyes full and looked at the man sitting in front of him.

"You all right, Son?" asked the man. He wore a blue uniform, and his round, beefy face was familiar.

Robert Proctor tentatively moved his head, and discovered he was seated in a reclining chair, unharmed, and able to move his arms and legs with no trouble. He looked around the room, and he remembered.

The man in the uniform saw the growing intelligence in his eyes and he said, "No harm done, Son. You just took the last part of your driver's test."

Robert Proctor focused his eyes on the man. Though he saw the man clearly, he seemed to see the faint face of the sleeping girl in front of him.

The uniformed man continued to speak. "We put you through an accident under hypnosis—do it to everybody these days before they can get their driver's licenses. Makes better drivers of them, more careful drivers the rest of their lives. Remember it now? Coming in here and all?"

Robert Proctor nodded, thinking of the sleeping girl. She never would have awakened; she would have passed right from a sweet, temporary sleep into the dark heavy sleep of death, nothing in between. His mother would have been bad enough; after all, she was pretty old. The sleeping girl was downright waste.

The uniformed man was still speaking. "So you're all set now. You pay me the ten dollar fee, and sign this application, and we'll have your license in the mail in a day or two." He did not look up.

Robert Proctor placed a ten dollar bill on the table in front of him, glanced over the application and signed it. He looked up to find two white-uniformed men, standing one on each side of him, and he frowned in annoyance. He started to speak, but the uniformed man spoke first. "Sorry, Son. You failed. You're sick; you need treatment."

The two men lifted Robert Proctor to his feet, and he said, "Take your hands off me. What is this?"

The uniformed man said, "Nobody should want to drive a car after going through what you just went through. It should take months before you can even think of driving again, but you're ready right now. Killing people doesn't bother you. We don't let your kind run around loose in society any more. But don't you worry now, Son. They'll take good care of you, and they'll fix you up." He nodded to the two men, and they began to march Robert Proctor out.

At the door he spoke, and his voice was so urgent the two men paused. Robert Proctor said, "You can't really mean this. I'm still dreaming, aren't I? This is still part of the test, isn't it?"

The uniformed man said, *"How do any of us know?"* And they dragged Robert Proctor out the door, knees stiff, feet dragging, his rubber heels sliding along the two grooves worn into the floor.

# SEE HOW THEY RUN

## BY GEORGE HARMON COXE

◨ ◨ ◨

The bus stopped at the side of the road opposite the country lane, and as he waited for the door to open, Johnny Burke could see the farmhouse and the sea of parked cars in the yard beyond.

"It's going to be hot out there today," the driver said. "And, brother, I sure don't envy you any. When I go twenty-six miles I want to do it sitting down."

Johnny swung to the ground, leather carryall in hand. The smell of the countryside was fresh and fragrant in his nostrils, but he knew the driver was right. It would be hot. In the seventies now by the feel of it. He was right about the twenty-six miles too. Why anyone should want to run that distance had always been a mystery that not even his father could satisfactorily explain.

Going up the lane he remembered the farmhouse from that other trip, years ago, but he did not remember the yard. Like a picnic ground or gypsy carnival, with the relatives of the contestants milling around and laughing and eating basket lunches. Already there were some who stood about in track suits and sweaters, and Johnny Burke smiled a little scornfully. Coming here that other time with his father he had been thrilled and excited, but that, he realized now, was because he had been so young.

On the porch of the rambling farmhouse which had for this one day been turned into the marathon headquarters of the world, the hubbub of voices lay thick about him. Inside there would be places to change, for his father had told him how the furniture would be carted to the barn beforehand. Somehow this seemed as fantastic as the crowd outside or the race itself. Why should

138

the owner turn her house inside out for a couple hundred maniacs? A Mrs. Tebeau, the papers had said. And although she was seventy-three years old she had, with the help of her daughter, served as hostess to the marathoners for sixteen years, furnishing sandwiches and milk for all who wanted them.

He noticed the girl as he climbed the steps. She was standing a few feet away, talking to some man; a slim, straight, pleasant-faced girl, looking strangely out of place here with her trim, heather-colored suit. She glanced toward him as he stopped, and smiled, and it was such a friendly smile that he smiled back and felt a sudden tingling ripple through him.

"Aren't you Johnny Burke?" The man, moving forward now, was a lank, lazy-looking individual, all but his eyes, which were blue and quizzical and direct. "I thought so," he said when Johnny nodded. "I saw you at the Intercollegiates last year. That was a nice mile you ran. I'm Dave Shedden, of the *Standard.*"

Johnny shook hands and thanked him. Shedden glanced at a list in his hand.

"So you're the John Burke that entered this year? We thought it was your dad. This would have been his twentieth."

"He couldn't make it," Johnny said, and then, because he could not explain: "So I thought I'd come up and take his place."

"It'll take some running to do that."

"So I understand."

"And what about the invitation mile in New York tomorrow?"

"I'm passing it up."

"Oh? I thought that was supposed to be your dish."

Johnny began to dislike Shedden. There was an undertone of sarcasm in his words, a skepticism that Johnny found annoying.

"I'd rather win this," he said.

"Just like that?"

"Don't you think I can?"

"Could be." Shedden shrugged. "Only you're stepping

out of your class, aren't you? You won't be running against a select little group of college boys today."

Johnny gave him back his sardonic grin. "Select, maybe; but they all know how to run or they couldn't get entered."

"They've got reputations, you mean," Shedden said. "Well, out here a guy needs more than that. It's pretty tough on prima donnas."

Johnny let it go and would have moved on had it not been for a sturdy, bronzed man of forty-five or so who bustled up to take the reporter's arm.

"Hey, Dave, where's Burke? You seen Burke anywhere?"

"This is Burke," said Shedden, and Johnny saw the man's wide-eyed glance and then his grin.

"Johnny Burke!" He was pumping Johnny's hand now and slapping his shoulder. "Young Johnny, huh? I'm Tom Reynolds. I've run with your old man for nineteen years. Did he ever tell you? Where is he? Is he quittin'? Old age getting him? . . . Oh, Kay."

And then, miraculously, the girl Johnny had been watching was standing in front of him. Her hand was firm and warm in his and he saw that there were auburn lights in her dark hair, that her nose was cute and lightly freckled.

"I saw you in the meet at the Garden two years ago," she said. "And I think it's grand, your running in place of your father today. He wanted to make it twenty races in a row, didn't he? And I heard what you said to Mr. Shedden about the race in New York. Will you mind so awfully?"

Johnny Burke said he wouldn't. He was used to the idea now, but two weeks ago it had been different. He had not known until then that his father would never run again, and he remembered too vividly coming down the stairs with the doctor that evening and going out on the porch where, with the darkness masking their faces, they had talked of Johnny, senior, and the verdict had been given. No more than six months, the doctor said. Probably not that.

It had been a bad night for Johnny, and before he fell asleep at dawn he knew what he wanted to do. His father, not yet aware how sick he was, had entered the marathon months before, and so, the next afternoon, Johnny told him he was going to use that entry and run this year's race by proxy and make the record an even twenty.

Even now he could see the thin wan face brighten as his father lay there in bed with the pillows propping him up.

"You will? You'll take my place?" he'd said. "Honest, Johnny?" And then, thinking, the doubt had come. "But that race in New York you've been talking about? That's the next day."

"The invitation mile?" Johnny had said. "What's that? I've beaten all those guys before, one time or another."

"You could win that race, though."

"I'll win the marathon too."

His father had laughed at that. "You're crazy! I only won twice in nineteen years and I was better than most."

"Ah, you were never anything but a fair country runner."

"I could outrun you the best day you ever saw," his father had cracked, and Johnny had jeered at him past the hardness in his throat because he saw how good it made his father feel.

There had been but two weeks in which to train, and he had worked diligently, following the schedule his father mapped out, wanting to cry sometimes when he saw how thrilled and proud his father seemed when he listened to the nightly reports. Johnny had worked up to twenty miles the day before yesterday, and when his father heard the time he admitted that Johnny might have a chance.

"Only don't try to win it, Johnny," he said. "This is no mile. You've been running races where only the first three places count. In this one the first thirty-five get listed in the papers."

Johnny hadn't argued then, nor had he told anyone the truth.

He knew how the newspapers would pounce on the sentimental elements of the story if they knew his father had run his last race. Not even his father must know that. And there was no sacrifice involved anyway. He had looked forward to that New York race, but he was glad to run this race instead, for he loved his father and knew how much this day meant to him each year.

He saw that Shedden and Tom Reynolds had moved on and realized the girl was waiting for him to speak. "No, I don't mind," he said again. "I've been arguing with Dad for years about this race and now I want to find out for myself."

"Arguing?"

"I can't figure it out. Dad has won twice, but in the past ten years he hasn't even been in the first five."

"My father hasn't been in the first five lately either."

"That's what I mean. Twenty-six miles, three hundred and eighty-five yards is an awful grind. If a guy feels he can't win——"

"You think no one should enter unless he feels he can win?"

"Not unless he's young and on the way up. There's maybe a dozen runners in the bunch. The rest of it's a farce." She looked at him strangely, but he did not notice and waved his hand to include the yard and farmhouse. "Look at them," he said, and in his laugh there was something superior, unconscious perhaps, but noticeable, for his was the viewpoint of one who has been at the top. "Anybody can get in that mails an entry. Anybody."

"Yes," Kay Reynolds said. "It's a poor man's race. You don't have to go to college or belong to any club, and there's nothing in it but a medal and a cup if you win. And yet they've been running this race for over forty years. There have been marathons ever since the Greeks defeated the Persians."

"Sure," Johnny said. "But why do they let all the clowns in? I read in the paper about some of them that even smoke——"

"Benny 'Cigars' Kelly and Jim 'Tobacco' Lane."

"Yes," Johnny said. "And the papers say they flatfoot the whole distance, puffing cigars and making faces at the crowd."

"Yes," Kay Reynolds said, "there are clowns. There always are in any event that's truly open. And there is Clarence De Mar, who is fifty-two and has won seven times. And Kennedy. He's fifty-seven. He's run twenty-eight times and finished twenty-seven races. And Semple, who's been running for twenty-four years. And your father and mine. That's why the papers call this race the biggest and freest sport spectacle on earth. Did you ever run before a half-million people?"

Johnny looked at her then. Her eyes were steady now and she wasn't smiling. "That's a lot of people," he said, and grinned. "Let's settle for a spectacle."

"But still a little beneath you."

Johnny's grin went away and his cheeks got hot. Who did she think she was, bawling him out? "What difference does it make? If a couple hundred fellows want to come out and run twenty-six miles, that's their business. I didn't come up here to make a spectacle; I came to win a race."

"Yes," the girl said, not looking at him now, and distance in her voice. "And I can see why you think you will. You've had every advantage, haven't you? The best coaches, and trainers and special food and privileges and expense money. These others have nothing but enthusiasm and determination. They are self-taught and trained and what food they get they work for six days a week."

"Okay," said Johnny, "I'm a snob. I came up to run this race, but I don't have to like it." He turned away, stopped to say stiffly: "It's nice to know you'll be rooting for me."

"I will," Kay Reynolds said, "because I'll be remembering your father, like thousands of others. I only hope you can do as well today as he would if he were here."

Johnny went inside, red-faced and angry, and the sight that met his eyes served only to heighten the irritation and bear out his argument. Like a side show at the circus. Skins of every shade from skim milk to chocolate.

Fuzzy-chinned kids, gray-thatched and bald-topped oldsters; fat boys with pillow stomachs and skinny ones with pipestem legs.

He made his way into a side room that smelled of wintergreen oil and stale perspiration and old shoes. He found a place to sit down and began to change, not listening to the babble about him until someone addressed him.

"Your first race?" The thin Yankee drawl came from a blond, shaggy-haired fellow beside him. "It's my fifth. My name's Bronson."

Johnny had to take the outthrust hand. "Burke," he said.

"Not Johnny Burke's boy?" Bronson's face lit up. "Hey, fellows! What do you think? This is Johnny Burke's boy."

They flocked about him then, fifteen or twenty of them, shaking hands and asking questions and wanting to know about his father and wishing him luck. And though he was proud of his father when he heard their tributes, he was scornful, too, because, of the group, only a few made mention of his own achievements; even then the others did not seem impressed, cataloguing him not as Johnny Burke who'd done a 4:10 mile but only as Johnny Burke's boy.

"I'll never forget him," Bronson said as they went out on the porch. "Hadn't been for your dad I'd never finished my first race. I was down around Lake Street, running about twentieth when your dad came up. You know they got official cars that have paper cups of water and lemon halves and things like that to hand out when you need 'em, but they're caterin' to the leaders mostly. And I think I'm about done when a car comes past and your dad hollers and they pull alongside to give him a cup of water and he douses it on my head." Bronson grinned. "I finished. Twenty-third."

Johnny looked at him. "Did you ever win?"

"Oh, no. Finished ninth once, though. Got me a medal for it. I figure to be in the first ten this year too. Look,

I'd like you to meet my wife. She's heard me talk about your dad——" He turned and was waving to someone, and Johnny Burke saw the sturdy apple-cheeked girl on the running board of a five-year-old sedan. She had a child on her knee and waved back. Johnny drew away, confused and a little embarrassed.

"Thanks," he said, "but hadn't we better get along to the starting line? Where you from?" he asked, to change the subject.

"Over Pittsfield way. Got a farm there."

"That's quite a jaunt, isn't it?"

"Oh, no. Lots come from Canada, even. We make a day of it. Start early, you know, and stop for a bite somewhere."

"And drive back afterwards?"

"You bet. Alice now, that's my wife, will ride along after we start and find some spot down around Brookline to watch the fellows go by; then she'll pick me up at Exeter Street after I finish. The official car'll have our bags all there waiting for us; and say——" He smiled with some embarrassment. "I guess you know a lot more about running than I do, but if this is your first marathon—well, I don't want to try and tell you, but don't let these front runners bother you. It's an awful long haul and——"

Johnny sighed. "I guess I can make out," he said, and then Tom Reynolds was there, looking bronzed and sturdy and fit, Johnny thought, like his father before that illness came.

"Been looking for you." He took Johnny's arm and drew him aside. "Don't let any of those fancy Dans fool you after we start. They'll dance away from the rest of us for three or four miles and then they'll get a stitch and get picked up by the Red Cross car and watch the rest of the race over a tailboard. They're like some of the other phonies."

"I'll remember," Johnny said, but Reynolds wasn't through.

"Your old man and I've been doing this for nineteen years. This was to be our last—we're no Clarence De

Mars or Bill Kennedys—and we're old enough to quit.
But now you've got to take old Johnny's place. Stick with
me. I know the pace."

Johnny nodded his thanks. "We'll see," he said. "I
never ran the course, but I think I can go the distance all
right." Funny. To hear them talk you'd think he wasn't
even going to finish without everybody helping him. "I'll
make out."

"Sure you will. And say, Coolidge Corner in Brookline
was always a bad spot for Johnny and me. That's gettin'
near the end, you know, with lots of autos around, and
not bein' front runners we couldn't always count on an
official car bein' near. So Kay's always been there since
she was a little girl, with lemon halves in case we needed
'em. She'll have one for you today." He paused and Johnny's glance faltered before the steady eyes because it
seemed as though Reynolds had read his thoughts. "But
maybe you won't need anything," he said abruptly. "Anyway, good luck."

The starter got them away promptly at the stroke of
twelve and down the lane they went, stretched clear
across its width and fifteen or twenty deep. To Johnny, it
was nothing but a mob and he moved out briskly to get
away from the dust and jostling.

By the time he reached the main highway he was running fifth and satisfied with his position, and for a while
then he did not think about the race, but only how he
felt. He felt good. Loose, with lots of juice in his flat-
muscled body and an easy animal grace that brought the
road back under him in long effortless strides. He didn't
think about his pace until he heard someone pounding up
beside him and then a voice in his ear.

"Easy, son." It was Tom Reynolds and he looked worried. "This is no mile."

Johnny nodded, a little irritated that this man should
tell him how to run. He shortened his stride slightly and
fell off the pace. Two chunky individuals went by him,
one young and one old, flat-footed runners, making it

tough for themselves already. Another came alongside, a string bean with pasty skin and a handkerchief, knotted at the corners, on his head, to keep the sun off.

He saw that Tom Reynolds was at his shoulder and thought about his advice. He thought of other things Tom Reynolds did not know about. He'd grown up knowing of this hobby of his father's, and how he trained, and hearing over and over the details of all these B.A.A. marathons. As a boy the race had seemed a colorful and exciting climax that he might sometime reach himself, but later, as he grew older and there were no more victories for his father, the idea of this annual contest had become an object of secret ridicule. Even his mother had sometimes acted ashamed in those last few years before her death. It wasn't dignified for a man of his age, she said. And what did he get out of it? It was probably the other women in her bridge club, Johnny thought, who asked her questions that she could not answer because she herself did not know why her husband ran on, year after year.

His own training had started while he was a junior in high school, and he could remember his father making him jog along with him sometimes, short distances at first, and working up in easy stages until he could do three or four loping miles without too much uneasiness. He had never lost a race in high school, and in college, though he was the son of a machinist and had to earn part of his expenses, he had become a figure of some importance on the campus solely because of the training his father had given him. That's why he was running today: to pay back a little of what he owed while it would do some good.

He saw now that they were running through a town and knew it must be Framingham. About five miles, he guessed, and he still felt good and there was no tightness in his lungs. There were crowds along the curbing now and he could hear them yelling encouragement up ahead of him. Then he was going by the checking station and from somewhere at the side he heard a roar that made him smile.

"Yeah, Burke," they said, and he waved back, thinking
of the times he'd heard that same cry in the Stadium and
Franklin Field and in the Garden.

He thought then of Tom Reynolds and glanced over his
shoulder. Runners were strung out behind him as far as
he could see, but Reynolds was not among them and he
knew he must have stepped up his pace while he had
been thinking.

Well, that was all right. There were other things Reynolds did not know. He and Bronson and those runners
who had shaken hands. Some had probably never heard
of him because they had no racing interest but the marathon distance; the others who knew of his reputation—
Shedden, the reporter, and Kay Reynolds included—did
not give him a chance. To them he was just another
miler, and a cocky one at that.

Perhaps he was. And this race was as he'd always
maintained in good-natured arguments with his father: a
bunch of screwballs out to make an exhibition of themselves for the most part, with a dozen or so real runners
in the pack. Well, he was running this one race and he
was going to win it and that would be that. What the
others did not know was that even while he was in college he had often trained with his father during vacations,
sometimes driving the car slowly behind him to protect
him from the other cars along the road, and sometimes
jogging alongside him, mile after mile. He knew what it
was to go twenty miles—he'd once gone twenty-five.
Today he was going to do twenty-six miles and three hundred and eighty-five yards.

He brought the race back into the focus of his thoughts
and found himself approaching the center of Natick with
perhaps ten miles behind him. Across the square some
enthusiasts had stretched a banner as a token of encouragement for a local contestant and as Johnny drew
near he heard his name called from the edges of the
road and found the tribute a cheerful sound, warmly
stimulating. But the race was already taking its toll of im-
pudent front runners. Of the dozen or more who had
been in front of him, seven had dropped out. Approach-

ing Wellesley he saw the pasty fellow with the handkerchief on his head sitting at the roadside waiting for a lift.

"Blisters," he said as Johnny went by. "Terrible blisters," he said, and waved cheerfully.

Along by the college the girls were out in force. Bright-faced, smiling girls in sweaters and gay skirts and saddle-strapped shoes. There would be girls like that in New York tomorrow night, and though he would not run he would be there for the meet and the parties and dancing afterward. He'd get the four o'clock down this afternoon, and Stan Tarleton would meet him, and with no racing tomorrow he could step out.

"Halfway," he said as he passed the checking station and took stock of himself and the race.

He was breathing pretty well, but he could feel his legs and the pounding of the pavement now, realizing that the roadbed was a lot harder on his feet than a cinder track. He lengthened his stride for a hundred yards to get a kink out of his right thigh and it went away all right and he dropped back to his former pace.

Between Wellesley and Auburndale two runners passed him and he let them go. Like the third quarter in a mile run, he thought, when it's still a long way to the end, but you have to keep the pace up. He was conscious of the heat now and it was harder to breathe. The pain was coming slowly, not real bad yet, but frightening when he counted the miles. Eighteen behind him. The hills of Newton and eight more to go.

The first hill seemed endless, slowing him down until he was practically walking at the top. Then, not sure how much longer he could go, he gained the downslope and his strength came back and he was struggling upward again. Gradually, as he fought that rise, a curious giddiness he had never experienced before came upon him and he did not know he was walking until he heard someone speak his name.

"Come on, young Johnny," the voice said. "Only a couple more hills to go."

It was an effort for Johnny to put the voice and the

tanned blond face together and then, through the curtain
of his giddiness, he knew it was Bronson, and picked up
his stride again to match the other. The car, coming up
from behind, meant nothing to him until there came a
sudden icy shock upon his head and the feel of water
trickling through his hair and down his neck. Then,
abruptly, his giddiness had gone and he saw Bronson
grinning at him, an empty paper cup in his hand as the
official car moved on ahead.

"Thanks," Johnny Burke said. "I guess it was the
heat." And he was both grateful and angry with himself
for not remembering that in this race there were ac-
companying cars and refreshments for those lucky
enough to get them.

"Sure," Bronson said. "Let's go now."

He started out in front, grinning over his shoulder, and
Johnny went after him, seeing the other draw ahead until
he realized that a country boy from Pittsfield was showing him his heels; then he pulled his shoulders back a
little and sardonic resentment at his near collapse kept
him dogging Bronson's footsteps all the way up the College hill and down the long slope to Cleveland Circle.

Here it was flat and he knew there were only five miles
to go. The pain was coming again and a numbness crept
along his legs and he thought, *It's like the last lap,* and
then a new and horrible awareness came to him and he
forgot the man up ahead. This last-lap pain for him had
never lasted longer than a minute or so; now it must go
on for five more miles.

"You went out a little fast, boy. You got anything
left?"

Tom Reynolds was at his shoulder, though he seemed
a block away. His face was twisted and set, too, but he was
breathing all right and his stride was firm and solid.

"Sure I've got something left." Johnny got the words out
one at a time, laboriously, angrily.

"Show me. Come on. Match me for a hundred strides.
Your old man could do it if he was here."

Anger drove Johnny Burke along for quite a while. He
matched Tom Reynolds' pace, forgetting the torture in his

lungs and the aching numbness in his legs. He wanted to talk back to this man who drove him on, but he knew he could not speak, and kept pounding on, not counting the strides any longer but always matching them until, somewhere down along the misty row of faces on the curbstone, Reynolds spoke again.

"This is the place," he said heavily. "This is where your dad and I always find out who's the better man each year. You're on your own now, Johnny Burke."

He moved out in front then, Reynolds did, an inch at a time, and Johnny saw the number on his back pull away and dissolve into soft focus. Somewhere, dim and thin and faraway, he could hear the voice of the crowd. "Come on, Burke," it said.

And he kept on, holding his own as a new nausea began to fasten about his stomach. Not cramps, but a simple sickness he could not understand until he realized that over the past few miles the poisonous smell of automobile exhausts had become much stronger as traffic increased. The thought that a contest must be run under such conditions infuriated him, and yet, even as he raged, he knew that this was but another hazard in the race to be shared by all who dared to try it.

For a step or two he ran bent over to see if this would help. There were more people here, he knew, and he could see some kind of square with shops and store fronts and streetcar tracks down the middle of the street. He staggered finally, fighting the nausea rather than his weariness. He looked about for an official car and found none near him. Then, his stride breaking now, he saw something loom out from the edge of the crowd. A hand found his and a girl's voice was in his ear.

"Suck on this," it said. "It's not far now. You can do it."

There was something in his hand and he put it to his lips and there was a tart strong taste of lemon in his mouth, laving his throat and starting the saliva again. He felt it going down his throat, the quick contraction of his stomach. He sucked greedily, breathing around the lemon, and gradually his head cleared and the nausea fled and there was nothing left but the pain and torment that come near the end for every runner who goes all out.

Someone drew alongside him. He could hear the slap of shoes against the asphalt pavement. The sound angered him and he pulled away, finding the strength somehow and knowing then that he was running better.

Up ahead he saw a bobbing figure and focused on it, watching it come nearer, drawing even and then hearing Bronson's voice as he went past: "Give it to 'em, Burke! Give 'em hell for me!"

Vaguely he remembered passing someone else, for the sound of labored breathing was not his own, and as he came into the approach of Kenmore Square he saw a familiar number just ahead and then he was matching strides with Tom Reynolds.

"Go on," the older man called, though it must have been an effort now. "What're you waitin' for? It's only a mile and you've got two ahead of you."

He saw them out in front as he pulled away from Reynolds. They were running shoulder to shoulder, raggedly, and he set out after them, blindly in his exhaustion, yet no longer worried or afraid. His running was detached, all but the torment of pain in his chest, and though below his waist there was nothing but fringe, he somehow found himself thinking with a curious clarity that explained many things in that last mile.

It was the cheering that started those thoughts. The sound of his name, like the pounding of rain, refreshing him, beating out a monotone of encouragement. "Burke ... Burke ... Burke!"

He remembered the cheering back in Framingham, the vague sounds of applause and enthusiasm that had accompanied him mile after mile. Not a brief, concerted cheer for a stretch run and victory that he had so often heard, but something new and different that he had never before experienced. For more than two hours he had heard these sounds, and the thought of this helped carry him now, filling him with wonderment until, struggling closer to those twin bobbing figures up ahead, the question came to him—how did they know him, this crowd? They had never seen him before. His name was in the papers' starting line-up. Number 18. Johnny Burke. And then, all at once, he knew. Those half million along the course who cheered were cheering a name, the memory of a name, the memory of other races back through the years. Not him, but his father, whom they had known and loved as a great competitor who always gave his best.

There were twin shadows at his shoulder now and the blood was boiling into his eyes along with the tears, and under his heart were red-hot coals. Loose bird shot filled his throat and the faces of the crowd went swimming by like painted faces in a dream. He lifted his elbows a little higher to give his lungs more clearance. He made a staggering turn into Exeter Street for the last hundred yards, and the sound of his name beat against his eardrums and he knew, finally, why his father had come back to run for nineteen years, why the others, not the clowns but the good competitors, came out on this day each year. Whether he finished first or fifty-first, each heard, for a little while, the sound of his name, a bit of acclaim to treasure secretly, to set him apart from his fellow man and make brighter an existence that otherwise was humdrum and monotonous; not an easy thing for any man to give up, for there is a need of such tribute in all men of heart and spirit, and each must find his little share in whatever way he can.

They said it was the closest finish in many years, but Johnny Burke did not know it. He did not feel the tape at his chest and would have run on had not strong hands grabbed him, supporting his arms so that he stood straddle-legged in the street with a sick stupor enveloping him until someone threw water in his face. Gradually then, the opaque shutter of his vision lifted and he straightened, seeing other faces about him and the cameras of the press photographers. When he felt someone prying at his hand he opened it and looked down and found the lemon, now squeezed to yellow pulp.

The reporters were kind to him as he stretched out on the white-sheeted cot in the basement of the old brick building. They stood about patiently until his heart had

slowed and the strength began to flow again along his
muscles. When he sat up someone put the laurel wreath
upon his head. He had to keep it on while the flash bulbs
popped, and then he had to talk, though there was little
he could say except that he was glad he'd won and knew
his father would be pleased.

Later, under the shower, he thought of all the things he
might have said, and of them all the thing he wanted most
to say could be told to no one but his father. He knew
how it would sound to those reporters—falsely modest,
pretentious; corny, they'd call it. How could he tell them
that he had not won this race alone, could not have won
but for his father? Oh, it was his legs and lungs that
did the job, but, faltering back there in the hills of Newton, it was Bronson who had pulled him through. Bronson, talking to him, getting water from the official car and
reviving him. Not because Bronson liked him or cared
particularly whether he finished or not, but because in
him he saw the other Johnny Burke. And Tom Reynolds,
taunting him into matching strides when he started to
lag again, reminding him always of his father so that
he would not quit.

These two who had helped him had been thinking of
his father, and yet, even with their help, he could not have
won without the lemon that stilled his nausea and comforted him. Now, letting the cold water play along his
spine, he had to know whether this, too, had been offered because of his father or whether that gesture Kay
Reynolds had made was in some part for him alone.

Upstairs in the corridors of the old clubhouse the
wives and mothers and families of those who had already
finished clustered about their men; others, still waiting,
gathered round to greet the front runners with the cama-
raderie born of good-natured competition. None seemed
disgruntled, and when Johnny Burke appeared they came
to him with their congratulations as though he had long
been one of them. He thanked them as best he could, the
cords in his throat tightening as he spoke of his father and
parried questions he could not answer.

How long he stood there he was never sure; he only

knew that it was an anxious time because always he was looking over heads and shoulders for a dark head and a heather-colored suit. Then, finally, he was by himself and an official had come up to ask him how the cup and medal were to be engraved.

"The way the entry read," Johnny Burke said, and the official, not understanding, smiled.

"But you're Johnny Burke, junior, aren't you?"

"Yes," Johnny said, and could neither explain nor say he wanted his father's record to read an even twenty races run. "Yes," he said again, "but I don't use the junior much. John Burke is the way I want it."

Then a soft voice was at his elbow, and his heart skipped and went racing on as he turned and saw Kay Reynolds' friendly smile. He had to clear his throat before he could reply to her congratulations, but there was a curious glow in his breast now; for as he took her offered hand in his he found something in her eyes that made him forget New York, something that told him from here on he was on his very own.

# POLAR NIGHT

## BY NORAH BURKE

📖   📖   📖

As the hot arctic summer drew to a close, till the magenta sun only slid along the horizon to sink again at once, the polar bear knew that a hard time lay ahead for her.

During the months of night, fifty degrees below zero, her cubs would be born. The great task of motherhood was already begun, the time soon coming when she would bury herself deep down under the snow to give birth. From then until the day when she and the cubs burrowed up into daylight again, she would not eat. She and they must live on what she had stored in her body during the summer, and on what she could catch and eat now. She must finish fattening herself up for the ordeal, and there was not much time left.

At the moment she was hunting along the edge of the ice, because where there was water there were seals, also fish, and the chance of a porpoise or walrus. As winter closed the roots and berries and lichen and seaweed of the polar islands into glass, the bears moved to the ice-edge for their food.

This was the arctic region, the area north of the limit of tree-growth. The shores of Greenland, Siberia, Alaska, Canada bordered upon this spectral sea. It was a landscape of snow and old ice and new ice, of drifting pack ice, and berg ice from the glaciers, all in constant motion, lanes and pools of pure cobalt looking-glass opening and closing all the time in the pack. Where the old ice had been pushed up together in terraces, ice-eaves burned green and lilac underneath. In summer the skuas and ivory gulls and other birds made the air raucous with quarrels, but now all that the bear could hear was the wash of blue water against grinding ice.

Under the dark sky, on the white land, in the desolation of the arctic landscape, she was part of its white power, moving with a long swinging walk and huge flat yellow hairy snowman footfalls. Strong and dangerous, the largest of bears, able to swim forty miles out to sea if need be, she stalked her kingdom in which no natural enemy challenged her reign. Her feet, bristled underneath to give grip on the ice, carried her huge weight with a light and silent tread; while the low swinging head searched the ice all the time for food.

She was not clearly aware of what was happening in her body, but the instinct was there to love the unborn cubs, to prepare for them and protect them; she did not risk her body in careless adventures as she would at other times.

But food? Food—

Already the iron of winter was in the clean cold air, though she felt the cold only with her eyes and black nose and black lips, where the air stung her, and on the long pinkish gray tongue, moving all the time to prevent freezing, that slung in and out of her mouth among the large cruel teeth.

Suddenly, away down the ice-field, where a dark blue lead showed in the pack, she saw a blackish slug on the ice—a seal. It was essential to catch him. In a moment she had decided on her approach, and slipped silently into the water to cut off his line of retreat. The ice rocked as her great weight left it.

The bear was as much at home in the water as on land—buoyant, swimming like a dog, but on top or submerged—and the water much warmer than the air on her face. Not wet, either: inside the layer of fat and the shaggy oily watertight coat, she felt as dry as on land.

By a series of cunning dives and approaches, and keeping under the shoulder of ice, she got near to the seal. Breathing carefully, every nerve keyed to the task of silent approach, ready to spring—to dive—to slaughter, she slid nearer—nearer—

Suddenly the seal saw her. Terror convulsed his face.
A moment of awful indecision—whether to plunge into
the sea, his natural line of escape, and perhaps fall
straight into her jaws, or to struggle across the ice to
that other hole—

He swung away from her, humping madly along. The
bear lunged up out of the water, on to the ice, on to the
terrified seal.

The water slushed off her everywhere like a tidal wave.
There was a flurry of snow and water and fighting seal.
His quick struggling body flapped under her as she slew
him. Blood spurted on to the snow.

When the seal was dead, the bear attended first to herself, getting rid of the wet from her coat before it could
freeze, although oil had kept off the frost so far. She
shook, and the drops flew off in rainbows in all direc-
tions. She rolled and nosed along in the snow, wiping
her flanks, her chin, and soon all was dry. A few hairs
crisped up and stuck to each other with frost.

Now for the seal. She ripped up the body, turning
back the skin and blubber, letting out a cloud of steam,
and ate greedily of the hot crimson meat. Seal meat was
her favorite, full of flavor, a hot meal, not like the white
icy flakes of cod.

Then, although the bear had no natural enemies, she
stopped suddenly as she ate, lifted her head, looked, listened, scented. Blood dripped from her chin onto the
snow.

There was nothing.

All the same she trusted her instinct and, leaving the
rest of the meal, slipped into the water, where she could
keep her cubs safe, where it was warmer, and easier to
move.

Presently she saw upright seals coming along the shore.
They were rather rare creatures, these, and dangerous
for all they were so weak. The places where they lived
had light and noise, and smelled full of good food. The
she-bear often drew near the places, attracted by those
smells. She hunted these land-seals too, and ate them
when she could. They were not like the sea-seals,

though. They wore seal fur, and their skins were rubbed with seal blubber, but there was a different taste inside.

They in their turn hunted bear, as the she-bear knew well. She had sometimes found the place of the kill, and seen the white empty skins hanging up by the camps, smelled the dark red gamy flesh cooking.

Now as she watched the approaching men, she considered whether to kill them, but the unborn life in her said get away. So she dived and swam and melted out of their radius.

In the next few days the bear gorged on fish and seal. No longer the hot rocks and scree of summer gave forth good-tasting moss and lichens or the sharp-fleshed berries and sweet roots. She dived into the cold blue ocean for her food.

But now the arctic day was over. In the pink twilight a snowy owl was flitting silently across the waste, moving south and south as life was squeezed out of the arctic desert by the polar night.

Then came the freezing of the sea. Crystals formed below the surface and rose, and needles of ice shot across from one to another, joining them together, thickening, hardening, adding more ice to the floes already many years old. The ice talked, grinding its teeth, sending out every now and then a singing crack. Curtains of colored flame rippled in the sky. The polar night began.

Now the real cold came. Now the food disappeared, and old male bears grew lean and savage.

The she-bear chose her den.

There was a great raw range of decayed ice that had been pushed up into mountains whose hollows were packed with snow. Icicles yards long hung on the south side from the summer, and behind this curtain of ice she found a great purple cave, carved in diamond and full of snow.

This was the place.

Her body was ready now for the ordeal. Thick fat, gathered from seal and halibut, lined her skin.

She burrowed down into the violet snow on the floor of the cave. It was so light that the wind of moving blew it about like feathers, and she could breathe in it. She burrowed deeper and deeper, while the snow sifted and fell in soundlessly behind her, till presently she was deep enough.

She curled and rolled herself round and round, pushing the snow, packing it, shaping the den. All the sides of it melted with her heat, then froze again into slippery walls. And the hot breath passed up through the way she had dug, melting the sides of the channel which also froze again and left a tube which would supply her with air until she came up in the spring.

Inside the snow and ice—inside her thick oily fur and the layer of blubber, she was warm, full fed and sleepy. She slept and waited.

In the fullness of time, the first familiar pang of birth trembled in her stomach. Pain fluttered like a butterfly and was gone.

She stirred, lifted her head, rearranged herself.

It came again, stronger, longer.

She moved uneasily.

Then in long strong accomplishing strokes it was there —hard, forcing, contracting, out of her control. Moving to a crescendo. She grunted, tensed all her muscles, pressed and gasped. Another spasm, and on the smooth strong river of pain, she felt the first cub come out.

A wave of relief relaxed her.

There he lay mewing, so wet and tiny, hardly alive, and she nuzzled him delightedly; starting to clean him up.

But now another spasm—the same long final one as before, though easier—and the second cub was born.

It was over now. She felt the diminishing contractions, the subsidence of pain, pulsing quieter.

Now to clean them up. She licked and licked them, turning them over, rolling and caressing them; then life strengthened in them as they dried, as they fed. She lay in bliss, feeling her own life flowing from her heart.

Meanwhile in the world above, the sun had returned, first a green glow, then a rosy one, then touching the topmost peaks, days before the first sunrise.

Deep in the snow cave, the bear knew it as the snow grew luminous with the light pressing through.

One day she heard voices. The snow vibrated with footsteps, the ice ceiling cracked.

She rose, shook herself free of the cubs and stood ready in case the land-seals saw the warm yellow air hole that marked her den—in case one of them walked over her and fell in . . .

She stood fierce, lean, ready, to defend her cubs, her heart pounding hot and loud as fever in her thin body.

Gradually the voices and the footsteps died away.

Presently it was time to come out into the world again. The cubs' eyes were open, their coats grown, they were walking, getting stronger every day. Now they must come out and face the world and swim and fight and catch seals. There was everything to teach them, and while they were still learning—still babies, they had got to be kept safe and fed. All this she had to do alone. Other years she'd had a mate to help her, but this time he was gone—lost— Those white skins hanging by the camps—

She began to tear her way out, the giant paws and black nails breaking open the ice walls of their den. The ice gave, snow fell in.

They climbed out.

Clean frozen air, dazzling with sun, hit them like the stroke of an axe. Light entered the brain in needles through the eyes. Only gradually, as the pupils contracted, did it become possible to see.

Under an iridescent sun-halo, the arctic landscape blazed white and navy blue. Everything hit them at once —light, noise, wind—the blast of a new world.

Down there was the water—

The mother bear plunged joyfully into the buoyant cleanness. All the dirt and staleness of winter were washed away. It was like flight. She plunged and rose and shook and plunged again in sheer joy. So fresh, so clean, the salt cold water running through her teeth—

Then she resumed the heavy duties of parenthood, turned to the cubs. They were sitting on the edge, squeaking with fright, and she began urging them to come in. They kept feeling forward, then scrambling back. Suddenly one ventured too far down the ice, and slithered, shrieking, into the sea, where he bobbed up again like a cork.

His brother, seeing this, plucked up courage and plunged in too in one desperate baby-jump, landing with a painful *smack!* and blinking in the spray.

They found they could swim.

Presently she pushed them up on to the ice again where they shook and dried, and the next thing was food. She left them while she killed a seal, and the three of them ate it.

After that there were lessons, how to fish, how to kill. Living was thin at first, for three hunters cannot move as silently as one, but they got along.

Until the day when land-seals approached them unseen from behind an ice ridge. The first they knew of it was an explosion, and one cub gasped and doubled up as he was hit. The bears dived for the water, even the wounded little one. He managed to keep up with them, and his mother and brother would die rather than desert him.

They all swam on, but slowly—slowly. Both cubs were still so small and *slow,* and they must hurry—

Blood ran in the sapphire water.

Other shots spattered beside them.

Anxiety roared in the she-bear's blood. Her heart was bursting. She pushed the cubs on, and turned to meet her enemies. Reared up on to the ice and galloped towards them, a charge that nothing could stop—not even death—if they'd stayed to face it, but they broke and ran.

The bear returned to her cubs.

The wounded one was sinking lower and lower in the water, breathing waves, and she managed to push him out at last on to distant ice. Then she licked him as he lay suffering in the snow, and his brother licked him too, whimpering with distress as he worked.

So that presently the blood stopped, and after a long time the suffering too. The cub sniffed the air. In the first real moment of recovery he consented to take food.

Pain went away from her heart.

Before them lay all the arctic lands, the snow in retreat. The floes, soft and friable from solar radiation, were being broken up by the waves. Plant life teemed in the water, the more open sea colored bright green by diatoms. Millions of wild flowers studded the rocky scree. There was everything to eat at once—lichen and moss and roots and halibut and seals. Salmon swam the green water, and cod. Seaweed washed round the rocks. On the land there were hares and young birds.

The summer gathered to almost tropical heat. Snow water dribbled into pools. Icicles glistened with wet, dropped and broke like glass.

And the mother bear, in the snow, with her cubs did not know why she behaved as she did. There was pain and there was happiness, and these two things drove her according to unfathomable laws. When the summer ended, and the polar night began, she would do the same things over again, and her children after her.

# THE TURTLE

## BY GEORGE VUKELICH

They were driving up to fish the White Creek for German Browns and the false dawn was purpling the Wisconsin countryside when they spotted the huge humpbacked object in the middle of the sandroad and Jimmy coasted the station wagon to a stop.

"Pa," he said. "Turtle. Lousy snapper."

Old Tony sat up.

"Is he dead?"

"Not yet," Jimmy said. "Not yet he isn't." He shifted into neutral and pulled the handbrake. The snapper lay large and darkgreen in the headlight beams, and they got out and went around to look at it closely. The turtle moved a little and left razorlike clawmarks in the wet sand, and it waited.

"Probably heading for the creek," Jimmy said. "They kill trout like crazy."

They stood staring down.

"I'd run the wagon over him," Jimmy said. "Only he's too big."

He looked around and walked to the ditchway, and came back with a long finger-thick pine branch. He jabbed it into the turtle's face and the snakehead lashed out and struck like springsteel and the branch snapped like a stick of macaroni, and it all happened fast as a matchflare.

"Looka that!" Tony whistled.

"You bet, Pa. I bet he goes sixty pounds. Seventy maybe."

The turtle was darting its head around now in long stretching movements.

"I think he got some branch stuck in his craw," Jimmy

164

said. He got out a cigaret and lighted it, and flipped the match at the rockgreen shell.

"I wish now I'd brought the twenty-two," he said. "The pistol."

"You going to kill him?"

"Why not?" Jimmy asked. "They kill trout, don't they?"

They stood there smoking and not talking, and looking down at the unmoving shell.

"I could use the lug wrench on him," Jimmy said. "Only I don't think it's long enough. I don't want my hands near him."

Tony didn't say anything.

"You watch him," Jimmy said. "I'll go find something in the wagon."

Slowly Tony squatted down onto his haunches and smoked and stared at the turtle. Poor Old One, he thought. You had the misfortune to be caught in the middle of a sandroad, and you are very vulnerable on the sandroads, and now you are going to get the holy life beaten out of you.

The turtle stopped its stretching movements and was still. Tony looked at the full webbed feet and the nail claws and he knew the truth.

"It would be different in the water, turtle," he said. "In the water you could cut down anybody."

He thought about this snapper in the water and how it would move like a torpedo and bring down trout, and nobody would monkey with it in the water—and here it was in the middle of a sandroad, vulnerable as a baby and waiting to get its brains beaten out.

He finished his cigaret and field-stripped it, and got to his feet and walked to the wagon and reached into the glove compartment for the thermos of coffee. What was he getting all worked up about a turtle for? He was an old man and he was acting like a kid, and they were going up to the White for German Browns, and he was getting worked up about a God-forsaken turtle in the middle of a God-forsaken sandroad. *God-forsaken.* He walked back to the turtle and hunched down and sipped at the strong black coffee and watched the old snapper watching him.

Jimmy came up to him holding the bumper jack.

"I want to play it safe," he said. "I don't think the lug wrench is long enough." He squatted beside Tony. "What do you think?"

"He waits," Tony said. "What difference what I think?"

Jimmy squinted at him.

"I can tell something's eating you. What are you thinking, Pa?"

"I am thinking this is not a brave thing."

"What?"

"This turtle—he does not have a chance."

Jimmy lit a cigaret and hefted the bumper jack. The turtle moved ever so slightly.

"You talk like an old woman. An old tired woman."

"I can understand this turtle's position."

"He doesn't have a chance?"

"That's right."

"And that bothers you?"

Tony looked into Jimmy's face.

"That is right," he said. "That bothers me."

"Well of all the dumb stupid things," Jimmy said. "What do you want me to do? Get down on all fours and fight with him?"

"No," Tony said. "Not on all fours. Not on all fours." He looked at Jimmy. "In the water. Fight this turtle in the water. That would be a brave thing, my son."

Jimmy put down the bumper jack and reached for the thermos jug and didn't say anything. He drank his coffee and smoked his cigaret, and he stared at the turtle and didn't say anything.

"You're crazy," he said finally.

"It is a thought, my son. A thought. This helpless plodding old one like a little baby in this sandroad, eh? But in the water, his home . . ." Tony snapped his fingers with the suddenness of a switch blade. "In the water he could cut down anyone, anything . . . any man. Fight him in the water, Jimmy. Use your bumper jack in the water . . ."

"I think you're nuts," Jimmy said. "I think you're honest to goodness nuts."

Tony shrugged. "This does not seem fair for you, eh? To be in the water with this one." He motioned at the turtle. "This seems nuts to you. Crazy to you. Because in the water he could cripple you. Drown you. Because in the water you are not a match."

"What are you trying to prove, Pa?"

"Jimmy. This turtle is putting up his life. In the road here you are putting up nothing. You have nothing to lose at all. Not a finger or a hand or your life. Nothing. You smash him with a long steel bumper jack and he cannot get to you. He has as much chance as a ripe watermelon."

"So?"

"So I want you to put up something also. You should have something to lose or it is no match."

Jimmy looked at the old man and then at the turtle.

"Any fool can smash a watermelon," Tony said. "It does not take a brave man."

"Pa. It's only a turtle. You're making a federal case."

Old Tony looked at his son. "All right," he said. "Finish your coffee now and do what you are going to do. I say nothing more. Only for the next five minutes put yourself into this turtle's place. Put yourself into his shell and watch through his eyes. And try to think what he is thinking when he sees a coward coming to kill him with a long steel bumper jack."

Jimmy got to his feet and ground out his cigaret.

"All right, Pa," he said. "All right. You win."

Tony rose slowly from his crouch.

"No," he said. "Not me. You. You win."

"But Pa, they do kill trout."

"So," Tony said. "They kill trout. Nature put them here, and they kill trout. To survive. The trout are not extinct, eh? We kill trout also, we men. To survive? No, for sport. This old one, he takes what he needs. I do not kill him for being in nature's plan. I do not play God."

Jimmy walked to the rear of the wagon then and flung down the bumper jack and closed up the door and came back.

"Pa," he said. "Honest to goodness you got the nuttiest ideas I ever heard."

Old Tony walked around behind the snapper and gently prodded it with his boot toe, and the turtle went waddling forward across the road and toppled over the sand shoulder and disappeared in the brushy growth of the creek bank. Tony and his son climbed into the wagon and sat looking at each other. The sun was coming up strong now and the sky was cracking open like a shell and spilling reds and golds and blues, and Jimmy started the engine.

Tony put the thermos away and got out his cigarets and stuck one in his son's mouth.

"So?" he said.

They sat smoking for a full minute watching each other, and then Jimmy released the emergency and they rolled slowly along the drying sandroad and down past the huge cleansing dawn coming, and the pine forests growing tall in the rising mists, and the quickly quiet waters of the eternal creek.